New Blood

New Blood

Peter McPhee

James Lorimer & Company Ltd., Publishers
Toronto

James Lorimer & Company Ltd. acknowledges the support of the Ontario Arts Council. We acknowledge the support of the Government of Canada through the Book Publishing Industry Development Program (BPIDP) for our publishing activities. We acknowledge the support of the Canada Council for the Arts for our publishing program. We acknowledge the support of the Government of Ontario through the Ontario Media Development Corporation's Ontario Book Initiative.

The Canada Council | Le Conseil des Arts
for the Arts | du Canada

ONTARIO ARTS COUNCIL
CONSEIL DES ARTS DE L'ONTARIO

Cover design: Clarke MacDonald

Library and Archives Canada Cataloguing in Publication

McPhee, Peter, 1957-
  New blood /Peter McPhee.

(SideStreets)
978-1-55028-998-5 (bound).— 978 1-55028-996-1 (pbk.)

I. Title. II. Series

PS8575.P44N49 2007   jC813'.54   C2007-904967-2

James Lorimer & Company Ltd.,
Publishers
317 Adelaide Street West
Suite 1002
Toronto, Ontario
M5V 1P9
www.lorimer.ca

Distributed in the
U.S. by:
Orca Book Publishers
P.O. Box 468
Custer, WA USA
98240-0468

Printed and bound in Canada

Thanks to Cindi M.,
of the S.E. Rocky View Anti-Bullying Project
for her help in researching this novel.

Chapter 1

The three of them walked slowly up to the school. To Callum, it seemed very new, though by its design and colour scheme it was clearly from the fifties or sixties. His last school was a dreary and imposing brick building built before the Titanic sank.

The main entrance was flat and wide, with large glass doors, a set of three broad concrete steps, and a wooden ramp for wheelchair access. To its right was a massive building faced with sheets of multicoloured concrete. Callum knew from the school's website that this was the auditorium and gymnasium. On the left were classrooms, rows and rows of glass windows surrounded by the same multicoloured squares of concrete. Above the main entrance was a huge hand-painted banner that read "*Welcome to a Brand New Year!*" Underneath in smaller letters it read: "*It's going to be the Best Ever!*"

Callum had his doubts.

Groups of kids were walking alongside them, yelling and laughing, pushing each other, all of them loaded down with backpacks looking full enough to climb Everest. Callum looked down at his own outfit — a Franz Ferdinand T-shirt, new jeans and old trainers, a vintage leather jacket he had picked up in a flea market back home. It felt odd to be wearing ordinary clothes to school. For his entire school life, he had always worn a uniform.

He could make out groups already, the Cool with their expensive outfits, the Jocks, the Geeks, the Goths and Emos, the nervous, the sad, and the not-fully-awake. Callum glanced quickly at his two friends and wondered how the three of them fit into the equation. Not Geeks, exactly; not the Cool, definitely; not Jocks either — that part of his life was gone forever. He remembered the noise of this many kids stuck together, the intensity of the energy they gave off. It was something he had nearly forgotten in his long recovery, the months spent absent from a schoolyard. He stuck his hands in the pockets of his jacket and took a deep breath, looked around, and plodded through the crowd toward the doorway.

Tyler was on his right, playing a game on his Gameboy; Aidan was on his left, buds in his ears, trying his best to look indifferent. When a few kids walked up beside them — some Callum had seen around the neighbourhood — they said a few words and drifted off again. Others openly checked out the new guy without saying a word. There were no attempts at introductions. The walk on the first day of school was not the time or place. It was a time to observe, to be seen, and to (hopefully) set the theme for the entire year.

They were at the unused wheelchair ramp when Aidan finally pulled the buds out of his ears and looked around, He glanced over at Callum. Tyler looked up for a moment, and then went back to slaying dragons, or ninjas, or whatever the game was today.

"So, Cal," Aidan asked, his mouth full of some fruit-flavoured gum. "How's it so far?"

"So far it's not that different."

"You ready? You psyched? What's going on?"

Callum shrugged and pushed his light-brown hair from his eyes.

"I suppose ah'm a wee drap feart."

"English, Cal, old buddy," Tyler said as he zapped aliens.

"I'm a bit nervous, I guess."

"It'll be fine," Aidan said and gave him a sharp push on the shoulder. "We don't have marauding killer gangs at this school."

Callum nodded. That wasn't what he was nervous about. He was nervous about a new school, new people, and a new country that didn't understand the way he spoke or his background. He was nervous about fitting in. The last thing he needed was to stand out.

They walked through the doors and into the main hall of the school. There were more banners inside and booths set up for various committees and school programs. There were groups determined to save whales, water, and the air. There were kids helping special-needs kids, muscular dystrophy fundraisers, others offering safety information on tattoos and piercings, STDs, anti-bullying, even labs for network game playing. A nervous looking red-haired girl was handing out hard copies of the school calendars "for the less-privileged who don't have Internet at home," she exclaimed.

To Callum's left there was a huge doorway leading to the auditorium. He peered inside, seeing a large, high-ceilinged room, the floors covered in gleaming hardwood and rows of fold-away benches against the walls. Retractable basketball hoops were secured by hydraulic shafts to the ceiling. Callum knew next to nothing about the game. To his left was a large stage, the curtains drawn. He shook his head at the large portrait of the Queen above it. *Some things never change*, he thought.

***

They sat in homeroom as the teacher, Mrs. Law, a middle-aged woman who loved to pronounce her words clearly and exactly, told them about the coming school year. She was quite tall, almost six feet, Callum guessed, with curly hair dyed black and colourful clothes slightly out of fashion. By pure coincidence all three friends had managed to get the same homeroom, and Callum felt a little relief at that. At least he wouldn't have to face the first few weeks at a new school alone in every class.

Mrs. Law droned on with the orientation and Callum looked around at the other kids, almost all of whom seemed nearly asleep at their desks. One person caught his eye in particular. She was a slight girl with thick wavy blonde hair and, from Callum's angle, at least, very pretty. She was intently studying something on her laptop and never looked up, oblivious to Mrs. Law's orientation.

"Now class," Mrs. Law said, her tone indicating that the orientation was over, "let's get to know one another, shall we?" Everyone straightened up a bit, getting ready for roll call and glad the speech was over.

"I see quite a few familiar faces out there, and a few new ones. I believe we have a new student here at Sir Winston High. Someone brand new to the country as well." Callum cringed as the others look around, all wondering who she meant.

"Which of you is the Scotsman?" Mrs. Law called out.

Reluctantly, Callum sat upright and raised his hand.

The entire class stared at him. *Not in a very*

friendly way, he thought. *More like an exhibit-at-the-zoo kind of way*.

"Stand up, young man, and introduce yourself," Mrs. Law told him.

Aidan, sitting directly behind Callum, gave him a shove and leaned over his shoulder. "Go on, my young Scotchman, stand up!" he whispered in a near perfect imitation of the teacher's way of speaking. Callum hated the ear-to-ear grin his friend wore. He stood up, shoving his hands into his jacket pockets to give them something to do besides shake.

"Well?" Mrs. Law said, as he stood there silently. He noticed that the pretty blonde girl was looking up from her computer and staring right at him. He wondered if he could blush any harder. "Introduce yourself, young man."

"Callum," he said.

"You'll have to speak louder than that to be heard. Come on, don't be shy. We're all friends here."

He cleared his throat. "Callum," he repeated, a little too loud this time.

"Your full name, please"

He sighed and tried not to think about the dozens of eyes staring at him. Callum took a shaking hand and nervously pushed his hair from his eyes.

"Callum McDuff," he said.

"Yes!" Mrs. Law said. "An actual McDuff here in my classroom. As you know, class, if you looked at your schedule, I will again be teaching English and Literature this year. Those of you who have had my classes before know that I am a bit obsessed with Shakespeare. I am also quite taken with the works of your own Rabbie Burns, Callum."

He almost winced at her attempt at a Scottish accent, and felt like telling her that the poet was not *his* Rabbie Burns.

Mrs. Law paused. She was waiting for him to reply.

"I see," he said in his best attempt at the Queen's English.

"Are you familiar with these two great writers, Callum?"

"Ah em, teacher," Callum replied, slipping back into his own accent.

"Pardon me?" she replied.

"Yes, I am, teacher."

There was a shifting in the seats and a few giggles in the room.

"Now, class," Mrs. Law said. "That is the proper way to address me where Callum comes from." She smiled at him. "You can call me Mrs. Law, Callum."

He nodded.

"Those who know me will also know my favourite Shakespeare play is *Macbeth*."

Callum felt his stomach start to churn.

"Are you familiar with it, Callum?"

"A bit, Mrs. Law."

"I happen to know a little about the British school system, Callum. I'm willing to bet you are more than a bit familiar with it. Can you recite a line or two from your famous namesake in the play?"

Callum looked quickly around and saw Tyler a row over. He was making a show of silently laughing and then holding his hands around his throat in a choking gesture.

"Callum?"

Callum looked back at the teacher.

"Turn, hell-hound, turn!" he called out.

There was more laughter. Mrs. Law was slightly taken aback but recovered quickly.

"Not exactly the quote I would have hoped for, McDuff," she said. "But it was accurate. I would like you to prepare a recital of a Burns poem. I have always loved to hear Burns spoken in his native tongue. I will pick the poem."

To Callum's relief, she indicated for him to sit. Mrs. Law started going through the class list and, when she was finished and everyone had had the pleasure of introducing themselves, the bell rang.

"Now, class, there are no formal classes today. The only obligatory event is Orientation in the auditorium. Try to behave yourselves and everyone have a great year. Welcome to grade nine!"

Callum couldn't get out of the room fast enough.

Tyler and Aidan were waiting for him in the

hall, still laughing. "Nice one," Aidan said. "Sucking up to the teacher!"

"I was not!" Callum shouted.

"Oh, come on!" Tyler said. "What was that 'yes, teacher' crap?"

"It's what we did at home!" His embarrassment was quickly turning to frustration. He knew they were just kidding him, but he wasn't in the mood for it. Not now.

"Hi, guys," a girl said behind Callum. He turned to look as Tyler and Aidan immediately shut up.

"Hi, Cin," they said in unison. It was the girl with the blonde hair.

"You're alone, huh?" Aidan asked.

"You see anyone with me?" she replied, her tone abrupt. Aidan shrugged and looked down the hall past the girl as if he was looking for someone. Callum saw that both of his friends seemed uncomfortable around the girl. She wore military-styled pants with lots of zippers, the cuffs reaching just past her knees. She had on a long-sleeved green shirt with a kind of vest thing on top. She held her backpack loosely at her side. As Callum's eyes moved up to the girl's face, he was startled to see that she was openly checking him over as well.

"So. Where is it you're from?"

"Scotland," Callum answered. He felt a little uncomfortable being so blatantly checked out by a girl. She stood fairly close to him and he saw that they were almost the same height. Up close she was even more attractive, with clear smooth skin and sky-blue eyes.

"That's cool. I'm Cindy." He almost lifted his hand to shake, but caught himself. He didn't know if you were supposed to shake hands when you met a girl.

"I'm Callum. Cal."

"Yeah, I heard. Old Lady Law is gonna make you suffer this year."

He nodded and didn't mention that he was already suffering.

"So how long have you been in Winnipeg?"

"A couple of months. We moved here in June."

She studied his face, a slight grin on hers. He prayed he wasn't blushing. What was she doing, this strange and intimidating girl?

"How did you hook up with these two clowns?"

"We live on the same street. They've been help-ing me adjust to Canada."

She was studying his face and he could see her lips move slightly as if she was reciting something silently.

"That's my street, too," she added at last.

Callum wanted to ask her where she had been all summer. He couldn't remember ever seeing her.

"We should go," Aidan said, "or we'll be stand-ing for Orientation."

"You gonna come with us, Cindy?" Tyler asked. He looked around again, scanning faces in the crowd. Cindy shrugged, hoisted her backpack onto her shoulder, and turned to walk down the hall. All three boys followed her. On the way to the auditorium they passed the administration offices and a wall of trophies, memorabilia, and awards given to the staff and students over the years. Callum noticed a curious office near the trophy wall.

"You have polis at the school?"

"We have what?" Cindy asked, craning her neck around.

He nodded to the office that had a sign on the door. It read *Winnipeg Police Service*. Below it was a small placard that fit into a slot on the door: *Constable Taggart on Duty*.

"Polis – police have their own office here?"

"Sure," Tyler said. "Every school has one."

Callum shook his head at the idea.

"What did you call them?" Cindy asked, slowing down to walk beside him.

"Call who?" he replied.

"The cops. Pole-something"

"Oh," he said. "Polis. It's what we call them at home."

She looked at him again, and again it was if she were reciting something. As they walked, Cindy closed her eyes and said, "Pole-iss. It's witt we caul them at haime." All of them turned to look at her, shocked. None of them was more surprised than Callum. She had performed a pitch-perfect imitation of his accent.

"That was pretty cool, Cindy," Aidan said. "How did you do that?"

"By observing. I decided that I want to be an actor when I get out of here."

"Cool," Tyler said. Callum wondered what she wanted to get out of — school or Winnipeg.

"So where's Rick?" Aidan asked her as she led them down the stairs.

"Is that what you're worried about?" she asked. Neither boy replied.

"Rick and I are just friends, okay? Always have been and always will be!" Then she added, speaking slowly for emphasis, "Nothing. But. Friends. Got it?"

Aidan and Tyler nodded, but Callum saw that neither of them believed her.

They finally reached the auditorium.

"Let's grab a seat near the back," Aidan said, peering in the auditorium doors.

"Nah," Tyler replied, "That's where the Jocks sit."

"So?" Aidan said. "We're grade nines now. We can sit where we want!"

"We may be grade nines," Cindy said. "But you haven't grown since grade seven."

"Funny," he said.

"Cindy!" a voice called out. "Wait up!"

Aidan and Tyler obviously recognized the voice. "Time to move, guys," Tyler said, turning away quickly. Aidan nodded and nudged Callum forward into the auditorium.

Curious, Callum looked back and saw four boys walking toward Cindy — four very large boys. One was in the lead, grinning and staring at Cindy. He was tall, with sandy-coloured hair done up in a faux-hawk, and a small gold bar pierced through his right eyebrow. The other boys had the same piercing. The boy in the lead tossed the football he had been carrying to one of the other large boys and rushed at Cindy, picking up her and her backpack as if they were stuffed toys. He twirled her around at arm's length and grinned up at her.

"Where were you all summer?"

"At my Aunt's," Cindy replied. The grin on her face was fading. It didn't help that a crowd had gathered to watch the scene. Aidan and Tyler halted just inside the auditorium, waiting for Callum.

"Why didn't you answer my e-mails?" the boy asked Cindy, still holding her in the air.

"I was busy, Rick. Put me down, okay?"

"Callum! Dude!" Aidan whispered. "Let's get a seat."

"Put me down, you idiot!" Cindy yelled, trying to hit Rick with her backpack.

Rick dropped her instantly and turned away from the crowd. His face was bright red.

"Sorry if I insulted you," she added, lightly touching his arm.

"What are you staring at, freak?"

Callum stopped staring at the scene before him

and focused on one of the large kids standing with Rick.

"You hear me? What you starin' at?"

It took Callum a second to understand what was happening. He was almost surrounded by four very large and very irritated older boys.

"It's okay. He's in my class," Cindy said, moving closer to Callum. "He just moved to Winnipeg."

Now Rick was fixed on Callum, his embarrassment turning to anger, and he now had someone to direct it at.

"So, tell me? Where you come from, is it okay to listen in on private conversations?"

"Rick!" Cindy began. He ignored her stepped toward Callum. The other boys started to move in as well. Callum stood his ground.

"It's okay, guys," Aidan said, walking up beside Callum. "We were just going into the Orientation, you know — the one with all the teachers?"

"Who asked you?" one of the boys shouted at Aidan, then quickly shoved him. Aidan flew back, his fall softened slightly by a group of kids as they scurried past, hoping not to get involved.

Callum felt his anger rise. "Lei hem alain, bassa!" he shouted, regressing into his own tongue.

The large boy made another quick move, this time toward Callum. Callum stepped aside smoothly and, ignoring the sudden spasm of pain in his right knee, kicked the legs out from under him. The large boy fell heavily to the tiled floor, hitting his head on impact. He rolled around, holding the back of his head, screaming in anger and pain. There was a moment of shocked silence as the crowd — and the other large boys — took in what had just happened.

Then they started toward him.

Callum was taken aback by how quickly everything had happened. Then again, it always happened quickly. He felt the all-too-familiar rush of adrenaline, the increased heartrate, and the shortness of breath. From instinct he glanced quickly around, checking exit routes, looking for something to use as a weapon. Wondering if anyone had his back.

Aidan was still on the ground, leaning on one arm. Tyler was nowhere to be seen.

Cindy stepped between the boys and Callum.

"Enough, you guys! I told you, he's foreign. He didn't mean any harm."

"He sure managed to harm Mike!" Rick shouted, indicating his friend rolling around on the floor.

"You think you can do some cheap move on our bud and get away with it?" one of the others shouted.

Callum didn't answer. He knew that the time for discussion was well past.

"Whatsa the matter?" one of the others asked Callum, faking some indistinct accent. "No speaka the English? Or maybe you're just some kind of retard!"

That comment got to Callum. He glanced at the giant boy lying on the ground, clutching his head and moaning like some overgrown baby. He looked at the crowd of silent kids staring and the large cavemen surrounding him, and he felt even more angry.

"I speak it a bloody-sight better than you, ya great big Ned!"

The large boy leaned back. "What the hell did you say to me?"

"I called you a Ned, and a wanker, ya bandy-legged grotbag!"

The large boy looked at Rick and the others. "Does anybody know what this little shit is saying?"

"Rick! Guys!" Cindy pleaded. "Enough. You're not impressing anyone."

She grabbed Rick by the arm and tried to pull him away, but he shrugged her off and walked closer to Callum. *This is it*, Callum thought. *How many shots do I get before I go down?* He flexed his fists the way his father had taught him and his feet automatically went into position, finding his balance. He was ready for the first lunge when Rick did something unexpected.

He pushed the others back and shouted, "He's mine!"

"Rick!" Cindy screamed. "I said enough!" She tried to get between Callum and Rick. All she did was block Callum's only chance at using the moves his father had taught him.

Rick rushed forward and grabbed Callum just as he had done Cindy, but with a lot less affection. He tossed him onto a table with a display warning of the dangers of Internet predators. Callum felt a sharp pain run along his spine as it collided with the tabletop and he was momentarily winded. Rick lost his grip and Callum rolled quickly and smoothly to the ground, feeling a sharp note of pain as he placed too much weight on the bad leg. He stood up and waited for Rick once more.

"Rick!" someone shouted, not Cindy this time but one of the boys. "Five-O!"

A gigantic man in a blue uniform, complete with a sidearm on his thick leather belt, walked briskly into the crowd. Constable Taggart, Callum assumed.

"What are you kids up to?" the constable asked, and Callum knew that he had sized up the situation before he opened his mouth.

"Nothing, Officer," Rick's friend said. "We were in a rush to get to Orientation and knocked the table over. The kid must have got in the way."

Rick was watching Callum. Callum kept an uneasy eye on him, knowing that he was still capable of another attack. The constable looked down at the upturned table and wrecked display, and then at Callum.

"Are you okay?"

Callum nodded, not taking his eyes from Rick.

"Look at me when you answer my questions, son," Taggart said.

Reluctantly, Callum looked away from Rick and stared at the policeman. "I'm okay. I was in the wrong place."

Callum saw the constable translating his answer. He straightened up and looked over at the four large boys. By now, Mike, the one Callum had knocked to the ground was standing, still rubbing the back of his head.

"Since you knocked it over, you clean it up."

They started to protest, but Taggart raised a hand. His other hand rested on his belt, right next to the firearm he kept in its holster.

"You can clean it up or you can go on report. The choice is yours."

Grumbling, the boys started to pick up the display.

"Okay!" Constable Taggart said to the others gathered around. "Show's over, kids. Let's get to Orientation, shall we?"

They all turned as a group and headed through the doors. Callum turned to join them, expecting that it wouldn't be so easy to leave. He was right. A large hand grabbed his shoulder. Callum turned to face Taggart.

"Is that what happened? You were just in the way?"

Callum nodded.

"You don't have to worry, son," Taggart explained. "We can look after you here. It wouldn't be the first time those boys have terrorized some-one smaller than them."

With that he looked over at Aidan and Tyler, who had mysteriously appeared once again. Callum looked at them and then at Taggart.

"I was just in the wrong place," he said. "That's all."

Taggart looked him in the eyes as if he knew what the truth was. He let go of Callum's shoulder and turned away.

"Holy!" Aidan exclaimed as they headed into the auditorium. "You totally stood up to those ass-wipes!"

Callum said nothing and Aidan turned to Tyler. "You saw it, right?"

Tyler nodded, grunting something non-committal.

"It was incredible," Aidan went on. "What was that kung fu move you did? That guy went down hard! And he's, like, twice your size!"

Callum was barely listening. He glanced over to see Cindy sneak away into the crowd.

"Where's the toilets?" Callum asked.

"Over there," Aidan said, nodding back the way they had come. Callum started to turn but Aidan grabbed him.

"You can't go back there. Those guys are prob-ably still cleaning up."

"Where, then?" Callum asked. Tyler nodded past Callum's shoulder.

"That way, to the left of the stage. It's where the

kids get ready before plays and stuff. There's a washroom there."

"What happened to you?" Callum asked.

"I was just stuck at the back of the crowd," Tyler explained.

"Aidan managed to stick with me."

"It's okay," Aidan added quickly. "Those guys have been beating the crap out of people for years. Tyler was smart to get out of there."

Tyler flushed. "I didn't get out of there. I just got stuck! And besides …"

Tyler had his cell phone in his hand, indicating it, about to say something more, when Callum cut him off.

"Forget it," Callum said quietly. "You weren't with us."

Tyler walked up to Callum. "What's that supposed to mean?"

Callum was still shaking from the attack and from adrenaline pounding through his veins. He wasn't in the mood for this as he stepped even closer to Tyler, staring up at him, daring him.

Tyler backed off, muttering, "This isn't where you came from, where you all think you're tough, supposedly carrying knives and slicing each other up for fun. As if!"

"You calling me a liar?" Callum asked.

"Chill, guys," Aidan said, stepping between them.

"No!" Tyler said. "Who does he think he is? If that cop hadn't shown up, they'd have beat the crap out of him!"

"Oh? So you saw that part, did you?" Callum said softly.

"Enough, guys!" Aidan shouted. "We have to stick together. It's us against guys like them."

Tyler and Callum glared at each other for a few long seconds before Callum turned away.

***

Callum rushed into the farthest stall after carefully looking around to make sure he was alone. He fell to his knees and vomited into the bowl, again and again, until there was nothing left but bile and his ribs felt like they had been pried apart. He slumped on the tile floor, his head resting against the cool ceramic of the tank, and tried to will himself to stop shaking. He pounded his fist against the wall while his other hand unconsciously rubbed the scars over his ribs. Then, as his breathing slowly came back to normal, he massaged his right knee, trying to rub the cramping and pain from it. At last he stood up, placing most of his weight on his good leg, and opened the stall door. He limped over to the sinks and ran his head under the taps. Callum jumped up when he heard a noise.

"We thought you fell in, Dude," Aidan said. Tyler stood beside him, still looking annoyed. Callum straightened up, trying to dry his face with the sleeve of his jacket and then the bottom of his T-shirt.

He wished he had fallen in.

Chapter 2

Callum ran up the steps of his brother's house, tore open the screen door, and rushed inside. He walked quietly down the hall to the basement stairs. As he did, he arched his back to relieve a bit of the pain and tightness running along his bruised spine. Before his foot could reach the first step, he heard his mother's voice call out.

"Callum? Is that you home?"

Callum sighed and headed down the hall to the small kitchen where his mother stood.

His brother's home on Morley Avenue was tiny, finished with old shingles and hardwood trim. Its best feature was a large backyard filled with lilac bushes and mature birch trees. It was only a two-bedroom, which did nothing to help the tensions forming with the merged families living within its cramped walls.

Morley was a narrow, shady street, quiet

despite being close to the city centre. Since he had moved here in the spring, Callum had rarely wandered far from this street, except for a few excursions to local malls or to the parks with Aidan and Tyler. Like his brother's backyard, it was lined with mature trees that formed a protective canopy over the street but somehow never managed to blot out the huge prairie skies that still captivated Callum after all these months.

In the kitchen his mother stood by the gas stove, stirring a huge pot. Another pot, covered but no doubt filled with potatoes, was bubbling away on the back burner. Callum knew what she was cooking and smiled wryly to himself. His mother turned away from the pot and lay her spurtle down on the plate provided for it on the counter. Her glasses were steamed up from the pots and she used a small towel to wipe them.

"So! How was you first day of school in Canada?"

She was grinning and looked rather excited, an emotion he rarely saw in his usually dour mother.

"It was okay, I suppose," he replied and looked past her to the pot on the stove. "Mince and tatties again?"

"It's your brother's favourite. And yours as well. What do you mean it was okay? Tell us, what it was like?"

"It was school, Ma."

She sighed and shook her head. "Did you meet some new people at least?"

Callum picked up the spurtle and began stirring the pot with it, staring at the ground beef and onions simmering in his mother's famous gravy. Large chunks of fresh carrot were the only bits of colour in the stew. He tried to think of something positive to say about his day. He couldn't tell her about his gyte homeroom teacher or the curious girl he had met. He definitely couldn't tell her about his encounter with Rick and his friends. His mother would probably demand they move yet again.

"What happened to your jacket?"

"Nothing. Why?" He laid down the wooden spoon and held out his arms.

His mother twisted him around so she could get a better view.

"Look at it. It's split up the back. And after you spending your own money on it."

Callum pulled it off quickly and checked it over. The seam had ripped and the leather gaped open, revealing the fraying lining. He swore softly under his breath. It must have happened when Rick had tossed him onto the display. He had loved the coat and now it was ruined. He was also a little annoyed his friends had let him walk home wearing it. He must have looked a right gowk.

"It's all right," he said. "It's too hot for here anyway."

"It gets cold here, too, Callum," his mother said.

Callum stared at the torn coat and, to his surprise; he felt tears start to well up. He felt silly and embarrassed. He was fourteen and he was almost crying over a stupid coat. It was as if everything he was, everything he had been, was slowly falling apart. Callum shut his eyes tight and took a deep breath to clear his emotions.

"Maybe you can sew it up?" he asked her hopefully. His mother took the jacket from him and lifted her glasses for a better look. She was an expert seamstress, something she had done for a living in Glasgow. She had yet to find work here.

"Sorry, son," she said. "The leather is too old and brittle. It'll just burst again if I put a needle to it."

He shook his head and walked past her. "I've got homework to look at," he lied.

"Homework on your first day? That's some school you're going to."

He wasn't sure if she was impressed or being sarcastic.

"What about your jacket?"

He waved back at her listlessly. "Just toss it in the bin."

"Teenagers!" his mother said to herself.

Callum headed downstairs to the makeshift bedroom his brother had fixed up for him. His room consisted of a beige Sears rug, a single bed, a dresser, and walls made from wide bamboo blinds picked up in Chinatown and hung from the joists. The basement ceiling was low and the floor was sloped and covered with crumbling concrete

— thus the need for the carpet. He pushed through the two blinds that made up his doorway and tossed his backpack on the bed. It was mostly empty anyway, containing a few books he had been given by teachers and the remnants of the lunch his mother had made him.

Before he had first arrived back in June, his brother had put up posters of Callum's favourite football (*It's soccer in Canada*, he reminded himself) team, the Rangers. Pennants and Callum's medals and ribbons, had surrounded the last team photograph of Callum when he played in the Rangers' junior team. Most of their stuff had arrived in Canada before them.

Callum had slowly taken the posters down and stashed them in the plastic containers that held most of the possessions from his past life. His football paraphernalia — old uniforms, cleats, trophies, and news clippings — were stored in still more plastic boxes lining the bamboo wall. The only things he had taken out permanently were his MP3 player and speakers, headphones, CDs, and clothes. With old bricks and some wood, he had made a shelf for his growing collection of books. His laptop took up residence on the small desk, the Internet connection and extension cord snaking away through his bamboo walls and upstairs through the heat vents. His favourite bit of clothing, the last thing he clung to from home, was now at rest on top of a garbage bin in his brother's backyard.

He slipped on the headphones and lay on his bed, letting the music numb his brain. His mind kept going over his first day at school — the large, pierced gorillas he had encountered, the pain of hitting the display, and the shame of boaging in the bathroom afterward. He thought of Aidan's valiant but doomed attempt to help, of how Tyler had faded away. He had to try not to expect too much from these friends. They didn't have the history he and his old friends had shared.

His thoughts were more distracted by Cindy, though. He remembered the way she shamelessly checked him out, the confidence she exuded, and the way she perfectly imitated his accent. It had been a strange day, with so much crammed into it. He thought of Cindy again, the curve of her leg beneath the knee-high pants, the clear skin and blue eyes.

Cindy, he thought. *Cindy*. He had never met a girl named Cindy before. Or a girl anything like her.

***

The wean is greeting.

Callum can barely hear him at first, but the crying gets louder. He tries to remember what happened, where he is. The wean is shaking him awake, calling his name.

"Callum!" the wean cries. "Get up! Callum!"

He lies in the dark, forcing his eyes to open,

feeling the cold earth beneath him slowly warm as something wet drains into it. He forces himself to wake, but the closer he gets, the more the pain floods in.

"Callum!" he hears the call again.

"Callum, get up here, son. Supper's on the table!"

Callum sat up in his bed in the bamboo room. His father was shouting down to him from upstairs. Sleepily, he looked around, almost as if his little cousin was still beside him, begging him to wake up.

Chapter 3

The five of them sat in the tiny dining room eating slowly. No one had spoken for a while and Callum was a little dazed from his unscheduled after-school nap. The mince and tatties, complete with a side of baked beans from a can, sat in front of him, barely touched as he tried to shake off the sleep and the dream he'd had.

"Where's your appetite tonight, Callum?" his mother asked as she delicately lifted another forkful of her meal. Callum was barely listening to her. He felt the familiar anxiety left over from the dream. He noticed that his back ached and his weak leg throbbed from his thigh to halfway down his calf. He was in great shape, in other words.

His father and brother didn't appear to be aware of Callum's lack of appetite. Both of them had tucked into the meal with a relish built from a long day at work. His brother Ewan, who was fifteen years older than Callum, had come to Canada nearly ten years before. In Scotland he had been an engineer, but didn't have the correct qualifications to work in Canada. He had become a tradesman, installing furnaces and heating systems, and after a while he found he was making more in the trade than he ever would have as an engineer. Their father, who had been an office clerk, was now his son's apprentice.

Both men looked very much alike: tall, with the sharp features, clear blue eyes, and black hair of their Celtic ancestry. Callum took after his mother, fair-haired, scrawny, and nowhere near as tall as his brother and father. He still had his hopes set on a growth spurt.

The other person at the table was Vickie, Ewan's wife of nearly three years. Like Ewan, she was tall and dark-haired, her pale green eyes easily sized up every situation. Ewan saw that she was moving the food around on her plate in pretence of eating. It wasn't exactly her type of food, he knew, and she had eaten even less than he had. Since the moment they had met, Callum had felt a connection with Vickie. He felt he could tell her almost anything without fear of criticism. She accepted him at face-value and spoke to him as an adult.

"You still haven't mentioned school," Vickie said. "What was it like?"

Callum shrugged. "It was okay, I guess."

"That's all I got out of him as well," his mother added quickly.

Vickie ignored her and pressed on. "What were the teachers like? Do you have any interesting courses? Do you have any friends in you classes?"

Callum shrugged some more. He didn't have an answer.

Vickie smiled. "Any cute chicks hit on you?"

Everyone laughed at this except for his mother. Callum smiled as the image of Cindy flashed in his mind.

"He's still too young for all that!" his mother said.

Vickie was grinning, knowing full well she was goading on her mother-in-law.

"I don't know. If I was ten years younger, I'd be hitting on him."

Callum and Vickie locked eyes, enjoying how this little exchange was irritating his mother's sensibilities.

Over the months Callum had noticed a strange rivalry growing between his mother and Vickie. It had started simply enough, with his mother offering to do the cleaning and the cooking since Vickie had to work all day. At first it had been great for everyone, but then his mother had tried to take over the household, preparing dishes that she believed were Ewan's favourites, despite the fact that she hadn't lived with him in years. Soon, it seemed that anything Vickie did wasn't quite as good as what her mother-in-law could do. The women were polite to each other, but Callum could see the resentment growing, particularly over the sticky-hot summer months. Despite the fact that the house had no air-conditioning, his mother was in the kitchen every day preparing the evening meals.

Actually, Callum had found that he preferred Vickie's cooking to his mother's. Before moving to Canada, the only hamburger he had ever tasted was from a fast-food joint. Vickie made thick, juicy burgers that his brother barbecued on the backyard patio. He had never experience the taste of broiled hot dogs, steaks, spiced chicken, and corn on the cob drenched in butter. He had never tasted a watermelon or fresh squeezed orange juice, or even a banana split or milkshake made fresh at the neighbourhood ice cream hangout. Mince and tatties were great, but they couldn't compare to beef ribs broiled slowly over mesquite, served up with baked potatoes and Vickie's homemade baked beans simmered with maple syrup and fresh apples. Not that he was dumb enough to ever tell his mother that.

None of the new arrivals had experienced anything like a hot humid Winnipeg summer, weeks on end with temperatures in the high 20s, and no breeze to speak of. They welcomed dusk and the slight coolness it offered, but that was when the mosquitoes came out. They had no immunity built up for the long, hot days, but what was worse was that they had no immunity to the tiny bugs. Mosquito bites left all three of them covered in large, painful welts that itched terribly, making it difficult to sleep.

Supper was over and, as usual, the two women had a polite dispute over who would do the washing up. Callum excused himself and walked through the kitchen to the back. He sat on the patio and closed his eyes, listening to the sounds of a Canadian suburb — kids screeching as they ran through a sprinkler, a lawnmower purring away, and traffic noises drifting up from Osborne Street. He still found it hard to believe how much his life had changed in the past year. One incident had changed the course of his life forever. Callum heard the patio door slide open and looked up to see his father and Ewan walk out, each carrying a bottle of beer. His father gave Callum a quick rub on the back of his head, deliberately mussing his hair, before sitting down on the chair next to him. Ewan took the chair across the table. Without realizing what they were doing, both men took a sip from their beer and sighed in complete synchrony before placing the bottle down on the glass-topped table. Callum had to smile at how much alike they were — and how different he was.

"Some life, isn't it, pal?" his father said, stretching his feet out and closing his eyes as he raised his face up to the warm evening sun. "Back home we'd be shivering, sitting out in the back like this."

"Back home you didn't have a back to sit in," Ewan said, laughing.

"I saw on the computer that it's been raining for over a week there," his father continued. "Flash

floods in Embra. Not that I feel sorry for that lot."
They all smiled. Embra was the Glasgow term for
Edinburgh, the capital city. There had always been
a rivalry between the towns.

"So what's up with you tonight?" Ewan asked.
The two of them had a wary kind of relationship.
Callum could barely remember Ewan while he
lived in Scotland. He had only seen him briefly in
the few holidays they had spent in Canada, and the
one or two times Ewan had come back to Scotland
to visit. He was more like an uncle or a cousin
than a brother, but they were getting to know each
other again.

"Nothing," Callum lied.

"Don't tell us that," his father added. "Come
on, spill it."

His father raised his thick eyebrows and Callum knew it was pointless to lie to him. He had
never been able to.

"It's nothing, really. Just too much new stuff all
in one day."

His father took another sip of his beer. Callum
noticed it was a Canadian brand. His father was
acclimatizing to the new country — faster than
Callum was, it seemed.

"What happened to your jacket, then?" Ewan
asked. "I saw it in the bin when I got home."

Callum shrugged. "It was old, I guess. It just
ripped."

"Just ripped? I see. So what's wrong with your
back then?" his father asked.

"My back? Nothing!"

"I saw the way you've been walking tonight. And I know what makes you not eat your supper and not babble on about your day. Lean forward."

That was the big difference between his mother and father. His mother saw the world the way she hoped it would be, his father saw the reality of things. Callum sighed and did as he was told. His father lifted the back of his shirt.

"That's some nasty bruises you've got there."

Callum shrugged away from his father's touch, pulling the shirt back down. He told them what had happened at school.

"You want me and your Ma to do something about this?"

Callum shook his head. He imagined things only getting worse.

"So how are you going to handle it?"

"I go to school and I stay the hell away from those guys."

"Exactly!"

"But if it happens again," Ewan added. "Let someone know."

Callum stood up and stretched his back, rubbing his aching spine briefly.

"I'm going to go for a walk, see who's about."

"Have you been doing the exercises the therapist gave you?" His father must have seen that he was favouring his right leg.

"Aye, Da," Callum lied. He had given up on the exercises months ago. He knew his knee was as good as it ever was going to be. He paused before going inside, not turning to face his father.

"Hey, Da? Ewan?"

"Aye, son," his father replied.

"You won't tell Ma, right?"

"You think we're that daft?" Ewan replied.

Callum smiled and opened the door.

"Hey, Da?"

"Aye?"

"Is it always going to be like this?"

Callum heard his father shift in his chair, heard the clink as the bottle was placed down on the glass table.

"No, son. It'll get better. I promise you that."

***

Callum walked down Morley using a fallen branch he had found as a walking stick, sometimes dragging it against the low picket fences he passed. He found he felt a little better after telling his father and brother what had happened. He was old enough to know that, just because his father said something, it didn't mean it would be so. He was young enough to hope that it could be. As he walked down the quiet street under a canopy of old trees, feeling the breeze of the late summer evening, Callum thought of the day and of the girl. When he got to Hay Street he turned left toward the school. It was deserted now, the wide lawns out front empty of the noisy, screaming kids rushing out just a few hours before.

He heard a whistle and some shouts coming from behind the school. Callum walked up Arnold Avenue toward the sounds. There, behind the school, was a huge field, with a large track for running, baseball and basketball fields. He saw that the football team was having a practice. Callum walked along the mesh fence, fascinated. The game was similar to rugby, but with a lot less physical contact and a lot more padding. Callum was amazed at how tall the students were, how massive they appeared in uniform and helmets. He watched the action until he heard a familiar voice. One of the players stood up and pulled off his helmet. The faux-hawk was slightly worse for wear and he was pouring sweat, but Callum recognized Rick instantly. He felt a familiar twist in his gut and he backed away from the fence, crossing the road and getting away from the field as quickly as he could. Only when he was back on his own street did he feel his breathing return to normal. Then he felt the familiar mix of guilt and anger. He hated that he was so afraid now. And hated himself for being a coward.

The joy of the evening walk had been sucked out of him, but he wasn't ready to go back to his brother's house just yet. He walked along Fisher to the small tree-filled park, hardly more than a patch of green space in the middle of the block. In the centre was a playground where small kids romped as young mothers sat chatting on the faded wooden benches, holding their coffee cups in one hand and their mobiles — *they call them cell phones here*, he reminded himself — in the other. Past the playground was a row of trees and bushes. Callum caught a glimpse of empty beer cans and cigarette butts. It was here, Tyler and Aidan had explained, that the older kids hung out, having parties until the small hours, drinking and making out in the relative privacy of the thicker bushes. There had been places like that in Glasgow, too, but they seemed a little more uncomfortable than this park. Not that Callum knew from any personal experience. As he debated whether to keep walking or to turn around — the muscles of his weak leg were starting to burn — his mobile chirped with a quick riff of a White Stripes song. He pulled the phone from his back pocket and flipped it open, knowing by the ringtone that it was Aidan calling.

"What's up?" Callum said in his best attempt at a Canadian accent.

"Not much. Bored. What about you?"

"Not much. Taking a walk. Bored."

"I hear ya."

There was a long pause and Callum quickly glanced at his display to see if the connection had been broken. He placed the phone back to his ear when he heard Aidan talk again.

"What?" he said.

"I said, what do you think of her?"

"Who?"

"Cindy. The blonde at school today."

Callum sat heavily down on a nearby bench. He rubbed the muscles of his right leg and flexed his knee a little. He stretched his back, trying to ease the tightness in his muscles.

"What do you mean?"

Even over the phone line, Callum sensed his friend's discomfort.

"I don't know. Tyler's liked her since, like, grade five."

For a moment, he felt a little twinge of something — guilt or jealousy, he wasn't sure which. He remembered Cindy all too well: the colour of her eyes, the blonde hair with highlights of copper and gold. He remembered her shirt, the way it fit her, and the knee-length pants with the smooth curves of tanned calves flowing down to new white trainers. Callum realized that the memory of Cindy was more vivid than what had happened a few minutes later.

"Oh, yeah?" Callum replied indifferently. "Has he ever done anything about it?"

Callum remembered the way Tyler had just faded away when he was being bullied by older kids. Was it Callum's problem if Tyler liked a girl and had never had the guts to tell her?

"Are you kidding? She's, like, totally out of our league! Besides, we all know the only thing Tyler relates to are his computers and video games."

Callum didn't want to talk about Tyler. "So that's why she's with that Rick scunner?"

There was hardly any pause — Aidan never asked him to repeat things in English.

"Who knows? They totally hang out a lot. For a couple of years now."

Callum shook his head. He wanted Aidan to get to the point, but he also wanted to keep talking about Cindy. He brushed away a mosquito. The parasites had found him.

"So what's she like?" Callum asked.

"Nice, I guess. Most of the time. She's, like, moody. You never know whether she'll even talk to you. Then sometimes she acts like you're the best friend she ever had."

"Why bother with her then?"

"You kidding? I mean, look at her! She's totally hot."

Callum laughed and brushed away more mosquitoes. He listened to birds in the trees, heard the buzz in the warm September air as the streetlights started to turn on. He agreed with Aidan. Cindy was hot.

"Besides," Aidan went on, "it's only since high school that she got all schizoid. She was pretty cool before."

"What happened?"

"Who knows? Her dad's home all the time now. Maybe he's on her case or something."

Callum knew that people changed all the time and there wasn't always a reason.

"Anything else?" he asked.

"Well, yeah," Aidan replied, hesitating.

"Maybe you shouldn't be so tough on Tyler. You don't know what it's been like for us, getting smacked around by those guys all the time. I guess they scare us, you know? Since we were kids."

"I don't know what it's like? So both of you think I made up all the stuff I told you?"

"Hell, no, Dude! I totally believe you! I mean, I saw the scars. You didn't get them from falling off your high chair."

Callum laughed at that. Aidan always seemed to say the right thing.

"Tyler believes you, too. It's just that he was scared. It's embarrassing to be our age and still be frightened of bullies, you know?"

Callum nodded, forgetting that Aidan couldn't actually see him. He stood up and swiped away more mosquitoes.

"Look, I better get back home. Anything else?"

"Nah. That was about it. Oh! Hey! You still there?"

Callum had just about flipped his phone shut, but he lifted it to his ear once more.

"Yeah."

"I, like, almost forgot to tell you. I sent you a link. You gotta check it out!"

"What is it?"

"Dude! Check it out. You'll love it!"

Aidan rang off and Callum shoved the phone back into his pocket.

He shook his head and muttered to himself, "What the hell was that?"

Back in his bamboo room, sitting cross-legged on his tiny bed, Callum pulled his computer onto his lap and started his browser. He clicked on the link attached to the e-mail Aidan had sent him and saw that he had connected to someone's personal blog. On the top of the page was a logo in a gigantic mechanical-looking font: SIR! WinsBlog. There was no indication of whose blog it was. Under the headline was a paragraph that read.

Hey, Kids and Cats! The new school year has just begun and it looks like the basketball team is off to a great start. Look at this amazing slam-dunk a certain R.A. completed in Orientation this A.M.!

Beneath the paragraph was a small widow for streaming video. Callum clicked the connection and a title came up — *The Flying Scotsman!* — It faded away and was replaced by a shaky, grainy video taken with someone's cell phone. He didn't recognize anyone at first in the large group of students milling about. On the audio, he heard a shout and the camera panned jerkily to the right. When it came back into focus, Callum saw a bunch of large boys converge on a much smaller one. His heart skipped as he recognized what was happening. He winced as one of the boys picked up the smaller one and tossed him heavily onto a table. Other kids ran in front of the camera and the scene snapped to black.

Callum looked up and sighed deeply.

He glanced at the e-mail Aidan sent and understood its subject line all too well now.

"Dude! You're famous! And it's only the first day of School!"

Callum shut down his laptop.

It was only the first day of school.

Chapter 4

On Wednesday the giggling began. At lunch Callum walked into the cafeteria and there were shouts and laughter from a few tables. A group of younger girls asked him if he'd had a good flight. But, other than that, his appearance on the *SIR! WinsBlog* hadn't made him famous as Aidan had predicted. Callum was very happy about that. He made it through the first week of school with no more embarrassing moments. Even Mrs. Law seemed to have forgotten her threat to make him recite Burns' poems to the class, although he was sure it would happen eventually.

He had seen Rick and his constant pals around the school, but, other than a few attempts to frighten him with sudden moves or insults about his mental abilities or sexual preferences, he had made it past them unscathed. The only real threat was Mike, the boy he had sent crashing to the floor. He had come up behind Callum a few times, blindsiding him and body-checking him into the lockers, and pile of younger students. It seemed that Rick had no further interest in him and, to keep it that way, Callum had decided to stay away from Cindy, even though he found himself thinking about her most of the time. All he could do was watch his back and try to make sure he was never alone. It felt like old times.

***

Saturday morning Vickie offered to cook, but Callum's mother insisted that they have her traditional Saturday breakfast of fried eggs, fried sausage, fried potato scones, and fried tomatoes. While they watched her cooking, Vickie leaned close to Callum's ear and whispered, "You don't think she'll find a way to make fried coffee, do you?"

Callum started to laugh as he was swallowing his orange juice, some of it spurting out of his nose, making the whole table laugh. His mother merely looked up from her frying pan and scowled.

"Why don't you make the toast instead of acting the clown?" she barked at him.

Callum reluctantly got up from the table, grinning and wiping his face with a napkin, his sinuses still burning from the juice. He grabbed the bag of bread and started sticking slices in the toaster oven.

"So what are you lot up to today?" his father asked as he sipped his coffee.

"Ewan and I are going for a drive," Vickie said.

His father nodded. "And you?"

Callum shrugged.

"I don't know. See what my pals are up to, I guess."

"Why don't you get your football out? It's been a while."

"Da!" Callum replied. "What's the point?"

"It'll get you some exercise. And some fresh air."

"I don't want to."

"Just do it. For me, okay?"

***

Half an hour later he was in the back alley, kicking his old football, letting it bounce off the hot concrete. After a few minutes, the movements rushed back, his muscles reacting instinctively to the weight and the physics of the ball. For a moment it felt like the old days, before he had been attacked. Getting cocky, Callum made a few quick moves, bouncing the ball off his knees, keeping it in tight control, occasionally kicking it against the wooden door of his brother's garage. Then he tried a little sliding kick, his patented move, slipping the ball under his left foot before quickly shifting it to his right. Then he attempted to flip it back over his shoulder. It was a move he had used to score goals when he was tight against the other team's net. This time, he forgot about his knee. He cried out as a sharp pain coursed along it and down his shin, making him lose control of the ball and his balance. He fell heavily to the concrete, skinning his elbows and shoulder. Callum felt a wave of anger at his clumsiness, at the skill that had been taken from him.

"Are you all right?"

Callum turned around, trying to scramble to his feet before his weak knee failed him again. He saw Cindy standing on the other side of the alley holding a plastic grocery bag. Callum's anger turned quickly to embarrassment.

"I suppose you saw all that?" He stood up, wiping the dust and gravel from his clothes. His knee and lower leg felt as though the ligaments had been torn away, but he managed a rueful grin and pushed his hair from his eyes.

"I actually used to be good at this," he said, holding up the football, trying to kid his way out of the embarrassment.

"I saw. You're still pretty good. You know, up until you fell on —"

"Fell on ma arse?"

She laughed. "And it's a pretty skinny one. It doesn't give you a lot of protection."

Now Callum laughed. When he thought about it later, he was flattered that she had actually noticed his arse — not so flattered that she thought he was skinny.

"I don't suppose I can comment on yours?"

"Not unless you want to get knocked to the ground again. Or at least until we get to know each other…. I guess soccer's pretty big where you come from, huh?" she asked, changing the subject after his long pause.

"Soccer's pretty big every place except here."

"Yeah, I guess hockey's the big game here."

Callum nodded and bounced the ball, keeping it under control without conscious thought. He had seen hockey on TV and thought it was pretty ridiculous — grown men skating around, wearing short padded pants and long socks, starting fights. He preferred seeing girls playing field hockey back home, their kilts flying.

"So how's Canada so far?"

He grinned and shrugged. "Still trying to figure it out."

She nodded, waiting for him to talk. When he stood there in silence, just bouncing the ball, she held up the bag.

"I guess I better get going before this stuff goes bad."

"Okay. See you."

"You're accent is getting better. I can almost understand you."

"Thanks," he replied. "I've been practising, watching a lot of Canadian TV shows."

"Poor boy," she said. "Well, see ya."

He felt a little moment of panic. He couldn't let her just walk away.

"Is it heavy?" he shouted to her back.

She stopped and turned. "What?"

"The bag. You need some help?"

"You look even scrawnier than me. What help are you gonna be?"

"I've been working out. And you're not scrawny."

"Oh? So what are you saying? I'm fat?"

He felt himself blush slightly. Girls had this way of twisting your words around. Callum took the grocery bag from her and was surprised at how heavy it was. She was stronger than she looked. They walked down the alley together.

"How did you hook up with Tyler and Aidan?"

"I was outside knocking my football around when they rode their bikes up."

"Sort of like what you were doing now?"

He nodded.

"Is that how you get people to talk to you?"

"It worked on you, didn't it?"

She laughed suddenly, covering her mouth as though caught off guard. Callum was thrilled.

"We just started talking. I told them I was having trouble setting up my computer and Tyler offered to fix it for me."

"Yeah," Cindy said. "Tyler is the ultimate geek when it comes to computers and video games and stuff."

Callum nodded. "We just started hanging out after that."

They walked on in silence again.

"So, you get over your introduction to Rick?"

He grinned and nodded. "I suppose. I know I don't want a repeat anytime soon."

"I was amazed how you stood up to him. No one does that."

"You did," he said.

She smiled and brushed her hair from her face in an unconscious motion.

"I've known him all my life. All of us have known each other forever, Tyler and Aidan, too."

"He seems like a great guy."

She looked up at him, at first to understand what he had said with his thick accent, and then to figure out if he was being sarcastic. She saw that he was.

"He actually is great once you get to know him. He'd do anything for you."

He nodded, wanting to change the subject. "Good," he said after a moment. She seemed to understand his mood.

"So. How about you? Getting used to us crazy Canucks?"

"I guess. It took me a while to figure out your accent and all your slang."

"Do I have an accent?"

"Sure you do. Everyone does."

"So am I, like, exotic?"

"I guess."

"It was a joke!" She nudged him on the arm. "Imagine me being exotic. As if!"

As they kept walking, Callum imagined he

could still feel the spot where her hand touched his bare arm.

"What kind of slang didn't you get?"

"Well, 'choked' for one. I had no idea what that meant. And 'dude' — it seems like everyone is a dude. Or stuff like money, like what's a dime or a quarter or a loonie. Calling petrol gas and drinks a pop, or scones pancakes. And expressions like, 'let's go downtown' or 'let's hit a movie'. Stuff you only hear in movies."

She was laughing again. "I never said 'let's hit a movie' in my life!"

"I was just trying to think of stuff."

"It seems so normal to me, but I guess it would be weird. I didn't know the way you spoke would be so different, though. I always thought you spoke English in Scotland."

"I thought so, too, until I moved here."

They reached the end of the lane and she nodded toward a house on the other side of Morley.

"That's my place," she said.

It was a small, neat house with immaculate shrubs and trees, and a lawn that was green and trimmed. He had passed by it a hundred times and never really paid it much attention. He remembered seeing a man working on the yard who seemed to deliberately avoid eye contact with his neighbours.

"I better take the bag now."

"I can carry it to your house. It's not that heavy."

She shook her head. "My dad's home."

"I'm not that scary, am I?"

He felt a twinge of disappointment, that their walk was over and that she seemed ashamed to let her father meet him.

"My dad doesn't let me hang out with boys. At least not alone with one. He says I'm still too young."

Callum nodded.

She took the bag and hefted it over a shoulder. "Thanks for carrying my stuff. See ya at school, I guess."

His mind was racing, trying to think of something to say, to make her stay a little longer with him. She walked away a few steps, then turned around.

"Hey, what are you doing this aft?"

"Nothing," he replied.

"Me and a couple of my friends are going to Polo Park."

"What kind of stuff can you do there?" Callum asked, imagining a large field with horses and upper-class twits knocking a ball with a mallet.

"You shop, Goof!" she laughed. "It's a mall!"

He was flattered that she wanted to do something with him. But the idea of going shopping with a bunch of girls was less than appealing. He was struggling to find a way out and to keep other chances open.

"Get a hold of your loser friends and get them to come with us." She paused for a moment. "If you want, I mean."

Callum was still mystified. He wasn't sure if his friends would be any more interested in going to a mall with a bunch of girls than he was. At least, if he went, he had a chance to talk to Cindy some more.

"I'll go see them," he replied.

"Okay. We'll be at the Osborne bus stop at around one, if you want to go. See ya!"

And with a wave of her hand she walked across the street and toward her house. He decided it was smarter to walk back down the alley rather than stand there staring at her.

Chapter 5

And so that was why the three boys stood waiting at the corner of Morley and Osborne, waiting for three girls so they could all go to a mall. Callum felt curiously nervous — or perhaps it was excitement — as he stood waiting, trying his best to look cool and collected. He saw that Aidan was the same way. Tyler was being Tyler, seemingly fascinated by the flyers stapled to a post. For once he had left his Gameboy at home.

Callum glanced at his watch as yet another bus came and left. It was almost one-thirty. Were the girls just late? Had Cindy played him? Was it just a joke to her? How long do you wait for a girl before you start to look pathetic?

"They said one, right?" Aidan asked as he grabbed Callum's wrist to look at his watch. Callum just nodded.

Tyler was crouched down looking at a poster

for a local band. "That's what chicks do. They make you wait for them," he said.

His tone was casual, as if he had any more experience with girls than the other two. Callum was about to suggest they just leave when he caught a glimpse of three girls in the 7-11 parking lot, heading toward them. Cindy was slightly ahead of the other two, and all three were whispering and laughing at something they obviously found intensely funny. Callum knew that Aidan and Tyler hoped as much as he did that they weren't what the girls were laughing at. Callum, Aidan and Tyler waited as the girls walked painfully slowly to the bus stop.

The three boys stood facing the three girls.

Callum recognized one girl with Cindy; she was in his homeroom, but he couldn't remember her name. She was smaller than the other two, with dark curly hair and olive skin. She was sipping through a straw from some kind of orange and green slushy drink. The other girl was nearly as tall as Cindy, with straight brown hair flowing almost to her waist.

"Hey, cool dudes," Cindy began. She nodded her head in a trying-to-be-cool movement. "Wazup?"

Aidan did the same cool kid nod, complete with a kind of ghetto signal with his hands.

"Z'up, my ladies?"

The girls started to giggle, but Aidan kept in character, folding his arms high on his chest and leaning back. Callum had to laugh at Aidan's perfect imitation of a B-boy.

"Girls, you know Aidan and Tyler," Cindy said to her friends. "This is Callum. He's the one I told you about."

The girls looked him over as if he were some kind of specimen — he almost thought they might ask him to open his mouth so they could check his teeth. Cindy introduced the girls to Callum. The dark-haired girl was Sarah, and the one with the fine brown hair was Brandie. Apparently, Brandie lived in the neighbourhood but went to an all-girls school in a different part of the city. Sarah moved closer to Callum.

"Say something," she demanded.

Callum just shook his head and shrugged. "What?"

"We want to hear your accent," Brandie added. Callum looked at them, then at Cindy, not knowing what to say or how to react.

"Gobshyte," he said at last, just to get the spotlight off himself.

Both Sarah and Brandie laughed at that. "Cool!"

"What did it mean?" Sarah asked.

"It's a kind of candy," Callum replied, straight-faced.

Before they could interrogate him further, an orange and yellow city bus pulled up in a stink of diesel and hot metal. They all jumped on board, swiping their student passes and running to the back of the bus. The three girls sat on one bench, the three boys facing them on the opposite side. As the bus pulled away from the stop, the girls spoke softly to themselves, their words muffled by the roar of the engine.

"So," Tyler said, speaking for the first time since the girls arrived. "What're you ladies buying at the mall?" He addressed them all, but Callum noticed that he was looking directly at Cindy. He remembered the weird phone conversation he had had with Aidan, about Tyler and Cindy. It seemed that his friendships might get complicated.

"Not much," Sarah said. "Makeup and clothes and junk like that."

"No one buying any sexy lingerie?" Aidan asked, grinning.

All of them laughed at that. Callum was impressed by Aidan's calm delivery. He wished he had Aiden's confidence in the presence of girls.

"Like, as if we'd tell you, perv!" Brandie shouted back at him, still laughing.

"You'd like to buy some for Cindy, right?" Sarah asked Tyler, giving Cindy a conspiratorial look. Callum felt a little twinge in his gut. Maybe Cindy liked Tyler after all. He knew that all these kids had known each other forever, and he had a lot of catching up to do. Tyler said nothing, just turned a little pink and looked away.

"What about you, Aidan?" Sarah continued. "Which of us would you buy something for?"

"Sorry. I don't buy girls' underwear unless

there's something in it for me."

Everyone laughed at this except for Brandie, who seemed confused.

"Eww! You'd wear girls' underwear?"

Everyone laughed again and Brandie looked even more confused. Sarah whispered in her ear. Brandie looked over at Aidan with a look of complete disgust.

"You *are* a perv!" she said, then laughed, unable to keep a straight face any longer. They all laughed again, and Callum felt the tension fall away from the entire group at last.

***

They spent several hours at Polo Park, where the boys mainly waited outside of stores for the girls, except for the music store where they all listened to samples of the latest releases. As they headed to the exit for their bus, they checked out the kiosks set up on the floor. Sarah was impressed by a set of jewellery, consisting of a necklace, bracelets, and little toe rings.

"Oh!" Sarah exclaimed. "These are so cool! I want them!"

"So buy it already!" Cindy replied.

"I don't have any money left," Sarah told her.

"So what?" A wide grin had appeared on Cindy's face. "Just stuff it into your bag."

"What?" Sarah said, shocked.

"Just take it. The geek clerk isn't watching us!"

They all just looked at her, amazed at her suggestion.

"You want her to steal it?" Aidan asked. Sarah looked at him, then back at the others as if looking for some idea of what to do next. When Cindy saw that no one was interested in her idea, she looked annoyed, then turned away.

"Suit yourself. I think they're ugly anyway!"

They all followed Cindy out of the mall. Callum was surprised, and a little disappointed. Where had that come from? Callum had been attracted to the fact that Cindy's behaviour was so unexpected, but this was going a little too far.

Four or five blocks away from where they had to switch buses, Cindy did another odd thing. She had been sitting on the back bench near Callum, talking to him and occasionally across him to one of his friends, when she suddenly jumped up.

"Let's get off now and walk home!" she yelled.

"The next stop is blocks away," Aidan said.

"So? We can pull the emergency line!"

No one said anything until Tyler jumped up.

"Yeah! I've always wanted to see if that actually worked!"

Before anyone could protest, he reached across the seat and pulled the cord. An alarm sounded and the bus driver braked immediately, pulling to the curb along Portage Avenue.

"Run!" Tyler shouted. They all followed him to the side exit and out the doors. When they were far enough away from the bus, they finally slowed down, all of them laughing at their little act of rebellion. Callum was glad for the rest. His right leg was already aching from all the walking in the mall and running had only aggravated it.

"See?" Cindy said as they slowly walked down the street away from Portage Avenue. "Wasn't that more fun that just getting off at the stop like everybody else?"

Callum started to see the advantage of the idea — it would give him more time with Cindy. But with his weakened knee and the heat, he regretted giving up his therapy routine.

"Which way do you want to go?" Sarah asked.

"Let's go up Broadway and over the bridge," Cindy suggested.

"That's too long!" Brandie said.

"No, it's not," Aidan said. "If we cross the tracks after the bridge, it's actually faster."

Everyone agreed, and the small group walked along the tree-lined avenue together. As the afternoon had progressed, a shift had taken place. At the beginning it was three girls and three boys, with a definite division between them. As the boys carried the girls' shopping bags, a new grouping was firming up. Tyler was walking with Sarah, Aidan with Brandie, and, still not believing his luck, Callum with Cindy. Callum glanced back and saw Sarah elbow Tyler in the gut, reacting to one of his bad jokes. The others were talking and laughing nonstop, but there seemed to be a lot of lulls in his conversation with Cindy. The silences made him uncomfortable. But she seemed calm, a slight smile on her lips. She pushed her light blonde hair from her face, looked at him, and smiled.

"Those four seem to be getting along," he said. He had no idea what to say to her and knew that she must be bored to death with him by now.

"I guess. They sure are noisy, though, don't you think?"

He laughed and nodded. They walked along in silence for a while, past the trendy shops and coffee bars along Broadway. The narrow sidewalk was filled with people — mothers pushing babies in strollers, couples with their designer clothes and designer coffees. The traffic noises were deafening at times, but Callum welcomed the slight reprieve from his inability to come up with anything to say. He felt hot and sweaty, his knee ached and his feet hurt from all the walking in his cool-looking but uncomfortable trainers. He was also mentally tired from trying to keep Cindy interested and make himself understood.

Callum looked up the wide avenue lined with ancient trees, their branches swaying lazily over the double lanes. At the intersection of Donald and Broadway there was a set of ugly, squarish fountains.

"Hey, Cal," Cindy shouted over the sound of the traffic and the fountains. "You wanna know a Winnipeg tradition?"

"Sure," he replied. All of them had stopped beside the fountains, enjoying the brief pause and the slight cool the spray gave.

"Every fall someone comes along and dumps soap into these fountains"

"Another thing I always wanted to do!" Tyler added.

"Yeah? What's the point?"

"It's tradition, Dude," Aidan replied. "There's no point to it!"

"Man!" Sarah shouted. "We passed a mom-and-pop back there. We could have bought some soap!"

"Look what I have," Cindy said, reaching into her purse. She brought out a small square box of soap, the kind they sold at laundromats.

"No way!" Brandie exclaimed.

"Totally awesome!" Sarah added.

Cindy ripped open the package and held it over the churning water. The traffic rushed by noisily on either side of the median, tossing her beautiful blonde hair about. Callum saw the look of total glee on her face, her wonderful smile, and he knew he was done for.

"Can you handle this?" she asked. Callum wasn't sure. He had never felt this way about anyone or anything before. The shock, the intensity of the emotion he felt as he stood there watching this perfect girl, her gold hair illuminated by sunlight, the tall elms soaring above her, the easy way she moved, made both of his knees weak.

"Do it!" Tyler exclaimed. Cindy started to turn the box over.

"Wait!" Brandie shouted. "Look at all these cars! What if someone calls the cops on us?"

"Come on, Brandie!" Sarah shouted. "What are they going to charge us with? Criminal sudsing?"

"Do it!" Aidan shouted. "It's tradition!"

"Yeah, tradition!" Tyler chimed in. Cindy slowly started to tip the carton over as they all chanted: "Tradition! Tradition! Tradition!" For Callum it seemed like a pagan scene, and he realized he hadn't felt this close to other people, so a part of something, in a long, long time.

The first few grains that fell from the carton were taken by the wind, but soon a stream of the white powder poured into the churning water. It took almost no time for the soap to foam, tossed around by the force of the falling water. It stayed at the centre, within the boundaries of the rough concrete, for a few seconds. Then, as it churned under the fountain's force, the suds rose up and in seconds were pouring over the sides, spilling onto the median, over their feet, and finally onto Broadway itself. The six of them grabbed handfuls of the soapy foam and threw it at each other, Tyler and Aidan rubbing it into the Sarah's and Brandie's hair. Callum and Cindy faced each, crouching with a load of foam in each hand. Cindy moved first, rubbing it in his face and hair, with Callum following her lead. She tackled him and he let her toss him to the ground. She straddled him, still rubbing the soap suds onto his face. No one stopped until they were all soaked and rolling around in suds. They looked around and saw that the suds had the traffic on both sides of the avenue slowing.

"Let's get out of here," Aidan shouted. They grabbed the girls' bags and ran across the road onto Donald St., still laughing uncontrollably. They passed a fast food joint and the boys all came to a halt.

"I'm starving," Tyler said.

Everyone else agreed. They started to walk inside the open door, past the fan on a tall stand that let a little fresh air into the store.

Tyler stopped and patted his pockets. "Hey, guys! I think I dropped my phone back there." He grabbed some money from his jeans and handed it to Aidan, asking him to order a burrito and a Coke, before running back to Broadway.

Soon they were all heading home again, taking a side street to avoid the noise and traffic of the main roads. Cindy's hair was drying in the warm sun and Callum noticed it was much curlier than usual. She was sipping a tall bottle of cranberry juice and occasionally she would grin at him, the straw still in her mouth. A couple of times she elbowed him gently for looking at her so intently. The silences between them were no longer painful — in fact, they were comfortable and seemed to bring a closeness.

"Why do you do that?" Cindy asked.

"Do what?" Callum asked, puzzled.

"Keep looking behind you. You worried someone is after you?"

"I was?"

"You didn't know?"

He shook his head. "Glasgow is a rough city," he told her. "It was always a good idea to be aware of who was around. I guess it's a habit."

"Well, you don't have to worry," she said as she wrapped her arm over his. "This is Canada. It's safe here."

She took her arm away, but Callum felt immediately better. Not about being safe, but about not boring her after all. As he smiled, thinking of her touch, he caught a glimpse of Tyler, who was staring at Callum. The look lasted only an instant, but both friends knew that something had changed.

***

Tired, hot, and sweaty, they made it back to their street at last. They walked slowly up Morley toward Cindy's house, the first one they would come to. The day had been perfect. Despite the pain in his knee and the heat, Callum reckoned it was probably the best day he'd had since moving to Winnipeg. Then two things happened almost simultaneously. Just as they crossed the street to walk Cindy to her gate, a car drove past. Rick was driving, and the car was loaded with three of his teammates, already dressed in their football uniforms for the game that evening.

As they reached Cindy's gate, they heard an

angry voice shout out. "Cindy! Where have you been all day?"

Cindy's father rushed along the path at the side of the house to the small group. He looked angry, almost in a rage.

"What is this?" he shouted. "What have you been up to?"

He opened the gate and stormed through. Callum saw that he was a lot taller up close. He was younger than his own father, and wore green work pants and a sleeveless T-shirt. Callum couldn't remember ever seeing an adult look as angry.

"What have I told you about being alone with boys?"

Cindy was pale. When she spoke, her voice was different, younger-sounding.

"I wasn't alone, Daddy. I had Sa —!"

That was all she had time to say. Her father reached out his right hand and slapped her on the side of her head. Callum heard the thud, knew the pain she felt as the hand connected with her ear. He felt another sick lurch in his gut — this time from fear.

"Don't you ever talk back to me!" He looked over at the others. "You! All of you, get away from my house. Now!"

They had already backed off, even before he slapped Cindy. Cindy's father grabbed his daughter by the hair, twisting her head painfully as he started to drag her back up the path. Callum felt anger overcoming his fear. He stepped toward the fence and yelled. "Hey!"

Cindy's father didn't even turn his head. Callum stepped forward, reaching for the gate, when Tyler grabbed him by the arm and pulled him back.

"What are you doing, man?" he asked, his face up close to Callum's.

"He can't get away with that!" Callum said, pulling free from Tyler's grip.

"Sure he can. He's her dad!"

"So what?" Callum replied, disgusted with his friend's cowardice. He had a quick vision of Tyler's disappearance the day Rick had attacked

Aidan stepped closer and grabbed Callum by the elbow. "What can we do, Cal? And anyway, it's none of our business."

Callum stepped back. He couldn't believe what he was hearing, couldn't believe how timid they all were in the face of what had just happened to a friend. He was outraged by Cindy's pain and humiliation.

"Have you seen this before?" he asked the girls. They shrugged, not able to meet his eyes.

"I guess," Brandie replied. "Nothing this bad."

How could they stand by and do nothing? Callum realized that he was close to tears, that his heart was racing. Without saying another word, he turned and ran. The others called out after him, but he ignored them, stopping when he was halfway down the block. His knee was on fire, the bones grinding together with each step. The scar running along his lower leg burned and the weakened muscles felt like they were stretched to their limit. He looked back at the sorry little pack of teens as they slowly dispersed. Before he turned his back on them, he saw Sarah pick up the plastic bag full of shopping that Cindy had dropped when her father had arrived.

***

Callum was lying on his bed, exhausted, nearly asleep, when his cell phone rang. Aidan again.

"What's up?" Callum said.

"Dude! We're famous! Did you look at the *SIR! WinsBlog* tonight?"

Callum told him to hang on while he clicked on the link in his Favourites folder. Nothing looked new since the last time he had looked. The bag of ice he had wrapped around his leg was now filled with lukewarm water and he tossed it onto the concrete floor.

"What am I supposed to see?" he asked Aidan, cradling the phone between his jaw and shoulder.

"Cal, look at the link on the top right."

Callum looked at the new tab, labelled *WINNIPEG TRADITIONS CONTINUE!!*

He opened it to see a short video showing the Broadway fountains foaming. The camera took in the whole scene in a shaky 360-degree panorama. A line scrolled along the bottom of the video, saying that the blogger had reason to believe that the soaping had been carried out by students from Sir Winston.

Callum grinned. At least it wasn't a video making him look stupid.

He and Aidan talked for a while, mostly going over the awesome day they had had with the girls. His anger with them had faded. He knew that there was little they could have done without making things worse for Cindy.

"Hey, Dude," said Aidan, "Tyler and I are meeting up with Sarah and Brandie tomorrow. Why don't you call Cindy and come with?"

"I don't think she'll want to see us."

"Why not?"

Callum shook his head. "After what happened, would you feel like hanging out?"

"Right. I'd be totally embarrassed. And pissed!"

Callum rang off, ready to sleep at last.

***

The wean is greeting.

Callum lifts his head and tries to open his eyes. They are sticky and it hurts to open them. The sunlight streaming through trees burns his eyes through the closed lids. He tries to lift his hand to shade his eyes and a sudden stab of intense pain makes him scream out loud.

The wean, his four-year-old cousin, screams too, tears streaking his dusty cheeks.

"Callum!" his cousin screams. "Get up! Get up afore they come back!"

"Patrick," Callum says softly, hardly more than a whisper. "Get my Ma."

"Ah cannie, Callum. I won't go. Ah'm too feart!"

"You have tae."

"Ah won't leave you!"

Callum realizes he is lying on the wet grass. He looks down and sees that his red shirt is soaked, clinging to his thin body.

Why did I wear a red shirt to school, he wonders.

Another wave of pain washes over him and he turns to his little cousin, ready to tell him again to find help. As he sits up slightly, using his elbows as leverage, it feels as though the air is sucked from his lungs. He can't breath. He reaches out to his terrified cousin, who shrinks back from his touch.

Callum sat up in his bed, trying to catch his breath, his hand rubbing his chest over the scars. He rolled off the bed and onto the carpet, feeling the cool of the concrete floor seeping through its fabric, gasping for air until his breathing returned to normal and the last shreds of the dream faded.

Slowly, shakily, he stood up, walked upstairs to the kitchen, and poured a glass of water from the cooler near the patio doors. As he gulped it down he looked at the clock on the microwave — just past four in the morning. He opened the patio door and walked out, sitting on the closest chair, not caring about the dew collecting on it. He glanced down at his pale, thin torso, illuminated by the lamppost in the alley. The worst scars lay across his left side, over the ribs and along a jagged path up toward his breastbone. The scars looked silvery under the alley light. He had other scars as well, on his back, his hands, and his leg. He kept his hair long to cover the slash across his neck, just under his right ear. That was where a lot of the blood had come from.

Callum laid the glass on the patio table and turned on the electric bug killer. He closed his eyes in its purple glow and listened to the faint crackles as tiny creatures flew to their deaths. He leaned back in the chair, legs up on the table, and closed his eyes, knowing there would be no more sleep tonight.

There was one difference this time. Instead, going over the moments before the attack and the waking up after with his terrified cousin looking down; instead of the months of surgeries and therapy, and the realization that he would never be the same; instead of the fear, he thought about Cindy.

Chapter 6

Callum walked quickly down the street toward school. He had the music on his MP3 blasting, trying to drown out the noise of the sea of kids surrounding him. For the first time since school began, he hadn't waited for Tyler and Aidan. He hadn't seen them yesterday; after the scene at Cindy's on Saturday he didn't want to. He really didn't want to see Tyler. Tyler's cowardice filled him with a curious mix of disgust and understanding. Logically, he knew that there was nothing he could have done about Cindy's father, but it still hurt that they hadn't even tried. He had considered talking to his parents about what he had seen, or his brother and Vickie. Perhaps they would know what to do. In the end he had kept silent, feeling hopeless, useless.

As he crossed the street, something caught his eye. He stopped and moved slightly into the alley to get clear of the flow of kids. Partway down the alley, he saw Rick and Cindy. She was leaning against a garage door, head down, holding her backpack against her chest. Rick seemed to be angry about something, gesturing wildly and yelling. Cindy never looked up. At last, Rick seemed to have made his point and started to walk away from her. Cindy grabbed his arm — from where Callum stood, it looked like she was pleading with him. After a moment he nodded, running a hand over his eyes, then smashing a fist into the garage door. He spun away from her and hurried off down the lane in the opposite direction. Callum backtracked from the alley, wondering if he should wait for Cindy.

"Someone should put that guy out of his misery."

Callum spun around at the sound of Tyler's voice cutting through the music still blasting in his ears. Aidan and Tyler had joined him watching the scene with Cindy and Rick.

Callum took the earbuds out and shut off the music.

"Dude, what was the rush?" Aidan asked

"What?"

"We shouted at you and you just kept walking,"

Callum just shrugged.

"You in a hurry to get to school to see your girlfriend?" Tyler asked.

"Leave it alone," Callum said. He glanced back down the alley but Cindy had disappeared. "Where were you yesterday, Dude?" Aidan asked.

"We met Sarah and Brandie up at Fisher Park, and —!"

"I had stuff to do with my family," Callum said, cutting him off. He started toward school and put his earbuds back in. He didn't know why, but he had no interest in what they did yesterday, only what they didn't do the day before.

"What's your problem, Dude?" Aidan shouted.

Callum opened his mouth, about to explain. Instead, he decided there was no point and kept walking. They slowed down and he left them behind. He was listening to the White Stripes, feeling a little better, still wondering what that scene with Rick and Cindy was all about, when he found himself falling forward. He instinctively held out his hands to stop the fall, but he hit the school parking lot hard; sliding on the loose gravel over the asphalt. The skin on his palms shredded painfully as his hands dragged across the rocks, only stopping when he rolled over on his side, his knee and right side taking the full impact of the fall. He rolled onto his back, frightened and angry, ready to spring up to attack his attacker. A large sneakered foot lunged forward, hitting him on the chest. He fell back onto the asphalt.

"Long time no see!" Mike said, grinning down at him. He had two of the other guys with him. Callum had yet to see Mike completely alone.

He reached out a hand to Callum. "Looks like you tripped. Want a hand?"

The other Neanderthals started to clap, and then

80

laughed as if the old joke was still funny. Callum straightened up, propping himself on his pained hands.

"What's the matter?" Mike said. "No fancy comments? No gay little kung fu moves today?"

Callum just looked past him at the crowd gathering to witness yet another of his humiliations. He wondered which of them was the creep with the camera and the blog. As he wondered, he planned an escape. If he could get up fast enough, he might make it past them, then over the fence into the teachers' parking lot and onto the street. He almost laughed at the ridiculous idea. Instead he looked up at Mike and told him to go try something anatomically impossible.

This time Mike had no trouble understanding him.

He kicked Callum in the ribs, and then spat on him. The three others placed more well-aimed kicks. Callum felt the wind rush out of him, felt the sharp spasms of pain rush through his upper body with each kick. He breathed hard and stared up at them defiantly. He saw Mike's face turn red — something snapped. Mike crouched down, grabbing Callum, and tossed him over the fence that he had planned to make his escape over.

The bullies stepped over the fence, and all Callum could do was brace himself.

He heard a voice, shouts as someone large pushed through the crowd. Callum hoped it was the police officer, or even a teacher. His heart sank as Rick appeared beside his teammates.

"What the hell's going on here?" Rick yelled.

"We're just having a little fun with the foreign kid," Mike said.

Rick looked down at Callum. "Good. I wanted to talk to him myself."

Mike and the others stepped aside, gesturing that Callum was all Rick's. Rick grabbed Callum by shirt, pulling him close.

"I saw you sneaking around, watching me and Cindy before. I'm going to tell you this one time. You stay away from Cindy! Got it? She's got enough problems without some little ass like you causing her more."

He slammed Callum against the wall, but Callum hardly felt the crash. It was as if Rick only wanted to scare him, not hurt him.

"I see you around her one more time and you're a dead man!" Rick said as he turned to walk away.

"That's it?" Mike asked. "We just walk away?"

"He got the point," Rick said.

"Yeah, but …"

Rick towered over him. "We've got practice."

With that, the others took Rick's cue and moved off. Callum tried to get up, but fell back down again, the pain in his ribs too intense. He rolled back onto the asphalt, feeling the gravel crunch under his back.

"Cal!" Callum opened his eyes to see Aidan and Tyler kneeling beside him. A crowd of other kids had gathered around. Sarah was there, her hand over her mouth, tears flowing. Tyler put his cell phone away to place a comforting arm over her shoulder. Aidan reached out and Callum grabbed his friend's hand, slowly getting to his feet. He took a deep breath and rubbed the spit off his cheek. His ribs were sore but he had felt worse. He shook off Aidan and started to brush the dirt from his clothes. Sarah grabbed his hands and looked at them.

"You have to see the nurse," she said.

They were bloody and scraped, with little bits of gravel and grass embedded in the wounds.

"I'm okay," he said. "I'll just wash them off."

He started to walk stiffly to the school doors and the crowd dispersed as quickly as it had appeared.

"Cal, Dude! You aren't still going to school after that?" Aidan said, trailing after him.

"What else can I do?"

"Report them." Tyler was right behind Aidan. "They can't get away with that."

Callum looked at him. "That type always gets away with it. How often did you report them?"

Tyler shook his head. "Look, trust us, don't go to school. Just stay away. The school won't even report you unless you miss at least three days."

Callum thought it over. He really didn't want to go to school. He was embarrassed and angry, and his body ached. He looked up at the blue sky. It was a beautiful day and he wanted to enjoy it. He nodded.

"Okay. But what can I do all day? I can't go home. My mother will kill me."

"Just hang. Go downtown, hit the malls. Whatever! It's a free day. Take it."

Callum grinned and nodded. Tyler and Aidan both slapped him on the back. Callum shut his eyes and held his breath until the pain subsided.

***

Callum lay on the banks of the Red River, sipping on a Big Gulp and letting the sun warm him. He still ached, but he had used the last of his cash to buy some aspirin to dull the pain. He still felt bad about skipping classes, but it was hard to feel too guilty lying in the sandy little bay he had found only blocks from school. He had his trainers and socks off, and his jeans rolled up. His feet dangled in the murky water of the Red. He looked around, feeling the breeze, listening to the wind rustle the tall trees, listening to the birds and insects. It reminded him of home, of the warm days he had spent with his mates wandering along the banks of the canals that fed into the Clyde.

Glasgow was an ancient city. The streets were narrow and dirty, everywhere were old brick tenements, and the sky didn't seem as large as it did in Canada. It was an old city trying to catch up with the modern world. Callum tried not to think of the life he had led there, the endless days when they would go to the carry-out for a fish-and-chips supper, washed down with an endless supply of Irn Bru. They would play football in the parks, in the street, all day and then head to Ibrox to watch the Rangers play. Callum had played on the junior teams since he was seven, and everyone had thought he had a chance to go pro. That all ended in an instant on a rare sunny Scottish afternoon, when he woke up to find his knee torn apart and his lungs gasping for air.

He put down the Big Gulp, a mixture of diet and regular Coke, wishing it was Irn Bru. Callum felt a wave of depression, a terrible feeling of homesickness for all that he had lost.

After a while he fell asleep under the endless Canadian sky.

Chapter 7

Callum came home at last, sore and tired. For once, his mother wasn't hanging about in the kitchen waiting for him. He ran down the basement stairs and threw his backpack on the bed before grabbing a change of clothes and running back up the spare bathroom. He took a long hot shower, aiming the jets at his tender ribs and running his hands under the spray to dislodge the collected bits of dirt in the cuts. He shut off the water and dried his hands gently. As he was pulling the last few bits of gravel from the cut there was a knock on the door.

"Aye?" he called out.

"You're supper's nearly ready," his mother yelled back through the door.

He entered the dining room, his wet hair combed back, wearing clean clothes and feeling a little bit better. At least his ribs and hands didn't hurt as much. The family was at their usual seats. Vickie grinned at him as he sat.

"Showering in the afternoon, are we?" she asked him. "Anything you'd like to tell us? Meet some cute girl at school?"

His mother sat at the table. "I hope not, so I do. You're far too young for the likes of that. And you're having problems as it is, fitting in here."

He looked up at her. "What problems am I having?"

"Just take yesterday," she replied after swallowing a delicate bite of food. Tonight was her attempt at spaghetti, featuring a pile of pan-fried meatballs covered in a can of sauce from the store. At least she was trying to change her menu, and everyone had to admit her homemade garlic bread was wonderful. "You didn't want anything to do with your wee pals."

"They probably needed a break, Ma," Ewan added. "They see each other every day at the school."

"What happened to your hands?" his mother asked. Nothing got past her, particularly anything to do with her baby son's health.

"Nothing," Callum said. "I just fell at lunch. We were kicking around a football in the back of the school."

"You weren't playing too hard, were you? I've told you to take it easy! That leg of yours is still on the mend …"

"I'm fine, Ma." Callum said impatiently, his

voice rising. "It's been over a year! I'm okay now!"

His father put his hand on Callum's arm and squeezed gently.

"That's enough, Callum. I won't have you raising your voice to your Ma!"

His mother leaned forward on the table, her food forgotten.

"You're okay now, are you?" she began, her voice taking on the calm, measured tone she always used when the subject of what had happened to him was raised. "I think it'll be a long time before you're okay. Before any of us are okay."

And then, to Callum's disbelief, she started to cry. She jumped up from the table and ran down the hall. Callum was shocked. He had never seen his mother show weakness of any kind. His father threw down his napkin and stood.

"You and I are having a wee word later," he said to Callum as he followed his wife. The three left at the table stared down at their plates.

"All I wanted to say is that I'm all right now," Callum said to no one in particular. Vickie leaned over, put her hand on the back of his neck, and gave him a gentle peck on the top of his head.

"You have to understand it from her point of view. No mother should have to go through what she did. Besides, you're her baby and she loves you."

"She's got a funny way of showing it."

Ewan sat up and turned to him sharply. "That's

enough out of you. Are you finished?"

Callum nodded.

"Then go to your room and keep out of sight for the night."

Callum stood up. There was more he wanted to say, more he needed to explain, but he knew it was pointless. He turned his back on them and walked down to his bamboo room.

***

Callum was lying on his bed with his headphones on, eyes shut, listening to the Silencers at full blast. He didn't notice his father had come into the room until he felt a hand on his shoulder, shaking him. He jumped and sat up slightly, pulling the headphones off. From the look on his father's face, he knew that he was in more trouble than he had expected.

"What's going on, Da?"

"I was just on the phone with the school. They say that you weren't there today."

Callum frowned. Why would the school call after only one day?

"I was going to tell you about that."

"That's not all they said. They said that you got into a fight with another boy. And somebody slashed his car's tires."

Callum sat up completely, slipping his legs over the side of the bed.

"It wasn't me, Da!" Callum protested. "You

know I don't touch knives."

His father shook his head. "I don't know what to think. You've not been in school a month, and already you're kipping school and getting into fights."

"Fights? That wasn't a fight! That was half the bloody football team kicking the shyte out of me!"

His father's face darkened. There was very little in the world that could make him angry. Someone attacking his son was at the top of that small list.

"What's been going on at this place?" his father asked, his teeth clenched.

"It's nothing, Da. The usual is all."

"The usual?" He grabbed Callum's hands and looked at the cuts. "Is this usual? Tell me how you got these."

Callum told him what had happened that morning.

"We can't keep letting this go on," his father said when he was through.

"What do you want me to do? Grass them to the school? What'll that do, except get them even more pissed? Besides, they're twice my size."

"You know how to handle that," his father replied. Callum nodded, but he wasn't so sure. The bullies were always together. Callum was always out-numbered.

In his youth, his father had been a semi-professional boxer and taught hand-to-hand combat in the British Army. He had trained both of his sons to take care of themselves in the dangerous streets of Glasgow. The problem was that, even if Callum could get Rick alone, he wasn't sure if he still had the nerve or the agility to fight him. He still woke up in tears, like a baby, after having his nightmares. His confidence was more than just shaken — it barely registered. The only advice his father had given him about being attacked by more than one person was simple: run! That advice hadn't helped him today, and it certainly hadn't helped more than a year ago when he had been surrounded in back of his semi-detached home playing with his four-year-old cousin.

"I don't know what to do," Callum said. "I don't want this to keep going on."

His father was silent a moment. "Then there's two ways we can handle this. The Winnipeg way or the Glasgow way."

Callum sighed. Neither option seemed great to him. The Winnipeg way would mean going to the school officials and getting a reputation as a rat. And even then, the school couldn't protect him every minute of his life.

The Glasgow way was simpler — the three McDuff men would take care of the bullies themselves. He wasn't sure if that would fly in Canada.

"Let me think it over," Callum said.

His father nodded and rubbed his son's back. Callum winced.

His father looked angry again. "Take that shirt off."

Reluctantly, Callum slipped his T-shirt over his head.

"The wee bastards," his father said as he saw the bruises covering his son's ribs and back. "If I ever see these Neds, I'll break their necks!"

Callum started to slip on his shirt again, but it hurt too much to raise his arms.

"You should have a long bath," said his father gently. I've got some salve to rub on you, stuff we used back in the army. It smells like middens and horse-shyte, but it works."

"Hey, Da?"

"Aye, son,"

"No telling Ma, okay? She'll probably move us to Alaska next."

"No worries there, pal. Mum's the word."

Callum stood up carefully. Lying on his bed had made him stiffen up terribly.

"How's she doing, anyway?"

His father shrugged. "She'll be okay. You have to know how it affected her, seeing you after. And you have to remember all of this is hard on us, but hard on her more. She's used to running her own house, her own life. Here she feels like an outsider."

"I didn't ask for us to move here," Callum replied a little defensively.

"I know that. We did it for us all. It'll be better once we get our own house, get her settled and meeting folk again."

Callum knew that his mother needed something

to fret over besides him.

"Maybe you should have a party, let her talk to some people other than us."

"That's not a bad idea. We could have a wee ceilidh. You can invite your pals as well."

Callum thought of his friends coming over to a McDuff ceilidh. With all the music and singing, it might be a bit overwhelming for them — not to mention how it would disturb the neighbours.

"I think that's a great idea. We'll plan for Saturday next."

His father turned and opened the slit in Callum's bamboo wall. "We'll talk tomorrow about all of this bullying stuff, see what we can come up with. Cover yourself up before going upstairs. And say goodnight to your Ma. I don't want you ignoring each other because your pride's hurt. You're a pair, you two."

Callum didn't like thinking he was that similar to his mother. His father slipped through the bamboo, and Callum winced as he reached over the bed to grab his robe.

***

Later, ready to go to bed, Callum heard his computer beep. He leaned over and hit the button at the centre of the keyboard. He thought about sitting up, but he still ached, even after his bath and the application of his father's salve, which smelled even worse than he had described.

He opened the e-mail and saw that Aiden had sent a link to the school blogger's website.

The splash page had the usual greeting: "Hey, Kids and Cats!"

This week's edition listed goings-on about the school, including videos of cheerleader tryouts, football practices, and various other events. There was an introductory note explaining each video in the blogger's usual goofy way. At the bottom of the page was another link with flashing lights and graphics of skulls and bones:

BREAKING NEWS!!!
A famous Jock by the name of Rick fumbled today after coming across heavy interference on his way home.
The poor Mr. Rick came across the torn and shredded corpses of some his favourite bits of inflatable rubber (besides his girlfriend).
Take a look … if you dare!!!

Curious, Callum hit the link and waited for the video to load. When it finally began to play, he was shocked. It was another shaky phone video. It panned across an older model car, the car Callum had seen Rick driving on the weekend. The camera sank down to show the slashed and deflated tires while funeral music played.

Callum shut down his computer and lay down on his bed. He wondered how the blogger had managed to get shots of the car. Did he see who slashed the tires? Had the blogger slashed them? There was no way of knowing. Callum tried to get comfortable despite the pain in his ribs and hoped that at school he wouldn't have to suffer too much humiliation.

Chapter 8

Callum and Rick sat across from Vice Principal Byrd. Officer Taggart stood beside her desk, arms folded, watching the two boys intently.

"I want to tell you, Richard, that I am truly sorry about what happened to you yesterday."

Callum had to think that over for a second. What had happened to Rick? It was his car that had been hurt.

"This kind of reckless vandalism won't be tolerated at this school. I assure you that, with the assistance of Officer Taggart, we will find out who was responsible."

Taking his cue, the large policeman unfolded his arms and moved a little closer to them.

"We managed to catch a glimpse of the person who slashed your tires. Unfortunately our cameras are at their limit on that side of the parking lot. This is the best we can do."

He showed them a low-res picture of someone, probably a male, standing near what might be Rick's car. Even from the grainy photo, it was easy to see that the vandal, a heavy-ish person with thick blonde or reddish hair, was carrying a knife in his right hand.

"I'm left-handed," Callum said.

Rick turned to stare at him. Taggart smiled.

"You noticed that, did you? It's obvious from this that you weren't the one who slashed the tires."

"How can you tell from that crappy picture?" Rick shouted.

"We can tell," Mrs. Byrd replied, sounding a little weary.

"Well, that doesn't mean he didn't have something to do with it."

"We wanted to ask you about that," Mrs. Byrd said. "What makes you so sure that Callum had anything to do with this?"

Rick sat back in his chair, not meeting anyone's eye.

"Is there some kind of problem between you two?" Taggart asked.

Neither of them spoke. Callum glanced over at Rick, who kept his eyes focused on the ground.

"I asked a question," Taggart said, his tone gaining an edge.

"Why don't you tell them?" Callum asked Rick.

"Why don't you?" Rick replied, daring Callum to rat out him and his buddies.

"Do you have anything to say to us, Callum?" Mrs. Byrd asked.

"Callum," Taggart said, when Callum just shook his head, "the school is aware of Mr. Atkins' reputation. You wouldn't be the first boy he and his friends have intimidated."

Intimidation? Is that what made his body ache? Callum felt his heart beat faster. He wanted to tell them everything, about the threats, the attacks, the fear he felt every day walking into the school.

"Nothing like that," Callum said at last. "He just doesn't like immigrants, I guess."

There was little more to say after that. Vice Principal Byrd finished off the meeting by reassuring Rick that everything would be done to catch the vandal. Seeing they were dismissed, the boys both stood up to leave, but Taggart put his hand on Callum's shoulder.

"Just one more thing," he said. Rick halted, looking at them. Taggart nodded toward the door.

"You can leave, Mr. Atkins."

With a final glance at Callum, Rick left, closing the door behind him. Callum stood near the door. The vice Principal cleared her throat.

"Now, Callum, we know you're new here and want to fit in. But Rick and his friends have caused problems in the past, and you aren't the first to be terrorized."

"It won't do anybody any good if you protect them," Taggart added, leaning in toward Callum. "He'll keep targeting you and others unless someone comes forward."

Callum crossed his arms and looked at the floor, sighing heavily. His ribs still ached terribly.

"I'm not protecting him," Callum said. "And unless you can watch him twenty-four hours a day, you can't do anything."

Taggart stood up to his full height.

"Fine. You can go."

Callum left as quickly as he could. Outside the office, he glanced in both directions to make sure Rick wasn't waiting for him.

He started down the hall to his first class, only fifteen minutes late. The halls were empty and his footsteps echoed along the tiled walls. As he passed the boys' washroom, the door opened and Rick rushed out, grabbing for Callum. Instinctively — and following years of his father's training — Callum twisted away and grabbed Rick's arm, throwing him off-balance. Rick stumbled and fell to his knees. Callum stepped back, ready for the next attack. Rick stood up, seeming a little embarrassed. He nodded toward the washroom,

"Get in. I want to talk to you."

"What is it? You and your girlfriends ready in there for me?"

Rick took a moment to process what he had said. "No. Just you and me."

Without waiting for a reply, Rick walked inside. Callum thought about running but knew it was pointless. He followed Rick into the washroom. Rick was leaning against the far wall, under a wide window with wires imbedded in the glass. Callum did as he had been taught — checked for exits and for anything to use as a weapon if he needed it.

"So what did they have to say?" Rick asked, looking as belligerent as ever.

"They asked me again to rat you out."

"And?"

"I'm no rat."

Rick nodded. "So you didn't slash my tires?"

Callum shook his head.

"You know who did?"

Callum shook his head again. "Sounds like you don't have a lot of friends."

"I've got all the friends I need."

He pushed away from the wall and stood up straight, uncrossing his arms. Callum braced himself as Rick walked slowly toward him.

"What are you doing with Cindy?"

Callum wasn't sure what he was talking about at first. "Nothing. I haven't touched her."

"You better not even try."

"Why?" Callum asked. "What's it got to do with you, anyway?"

Rick flushed. "It's got plenty to do with me. Just stay away from her!"

He pushed past Callum, heading for the door.

"Why?" he shouted to Rick's back. "Why does it matter so much to you?"

Rick turned, lifted a large hand, and pointed a finger at Callum.

"Just do like I say. You have no idea how I've been keeping my pals in control. Without me around, you and your little nerd friends would get stomped even worse."

Callum walked toward him. "Just tell me. Give me a good reason and I'll stay away from her."

"Okay," Rick began, his voice much softer, "this is between me and you, right?"

Callum nodded, almost grinning at the absurd notion that he and Rick were conspirators.

"Cindy's had it tough growing up, okay? She doesn't need some punk like you messing her up some more."

Callum was surprised — surprised that Rick could actually care about another human being, and surprised that he would think that Callum could actually have any effect on Cindy.

"I won't mess her up," Callum said, thinking that it was likely he would be the one who got messed up.

Rick looked like he was about to leave once more, but stopped. "How do you know that stuff?"

"What?"

"The martial arts stuff — making me fall over."

"Oh," Callum said, "my father taught me. He learned how to fight in the army."

"Cool," Rick replied. "Maybe I'll get you to show me someday."

"I don't think you need to know," Callum said. "You're big enough to not worry about it." Showing a huge bully how to hurt people even more would be a bad idea.

Rick opened the door and left. Callum felt the tension burst from him. As he ran water over his hands and face, he saw that his hands were shaking. The pain in his ribs suddenly rushed back. He dried himself off and headed out the door to class.

Chapter 9

The evening meal was quieter than usual that night. Callum and his mother were polite to one another, but still a bit wary after the previous night's blow up. After a brief discussion of the events at school and Callum's innocence in the tire-slashing incident, he excused himself to have another bath.

Callum was downstairs, not sure if he should go to bed or back upstairs to join the others, when he heard his brother shout down. "Callum! You awake?"

"Yeah," Callum replied. "Why?"

"There's someone here to see you. A wee stoater!"

Callum frowned, wondering what Ewan was going on about. He dressed quickly, ran a comb through his still-damp hair, and walked upstairs. He was more than a little shocked to see Cindy standing in the foyer. Ewan and Vickie stood there, smiling at him.

"Hey," Cindy said, giving him a small nervous wave. Callum was surprised — he had only ever seen her exude confidence.

"Hey," he replied. He hated the way that Ewan and Vickie just stood there, grinning.

"I tried calling your cell, but you didn't pick up. So I thought I'd walk over."

"Oh! I was just having a bath."

"He's been taking them every night," Vickie said. "Now we know why."

Callum just looked at her. Then he remembered his manners.

"Um, this is my sister-in-law Vickie and my brother, Ewan," he said quickly. "This is Cindy. From school."

They all nodded at each other, then stood there in uncomfortable silence.

"You're not like Callum," Cindy said to Vickie. "Foreign, I mean,"

"No," Vickie replied, shaking her head. "I'm from Transcona."

Another awkward silence was broken when Cindy suggested she and Callum go outside.

"So," Callum said, as they walked down the path to the sidewalk. "What's up?"

"Nothing, I just wanted to come see you. Maybe go for a walk or something."

"Sure," Callum said. His heart was pounding. They walked down the block away from both of their houses. For about half a block neither of them spoke. It was a clear, warm evening and a gentle breeze tousled Cindy's hair. She was wearing shorts and sandals, and yet another long-sleeved top.

"What did your brother call me?"

"When?"

"When he called down for you. He said someone was there, a real something."

"Oh, right," Callum said, remembering. "He called you a stoater."

"What's that? Some kind of rodent?"

Callum laughed. "No, that's a stoat. Stoater is a Scottish word for something really nice, really cool. You know, the English would say you're a cracker."

She laughed. "Oh, great! So over there I'm either a rat or a snack!"

"Or maybe a bit of both?"

They both grinned, and then there was that friendly silence again.

"I had a nice time on Saturday," Cindy said. "How about you?"

Callum nodded. "Sure. It was nice.

"Because of the mall or because of me?" Callum felt himself flush. He'd never had to answer so direct a question from a girl before. She laughed and grabbed his hand in both of hers. She leaned against him, her shoulders touching his before she leaned away. "I'm just bugging you, goof!"

He smiled at her, relieved that he didn't have to speak. She took one of her hands away, but the other stayed where it was, holding his as they continued down the street.

"I don't really like malls," he said at last, hoping she would get his meaning.

"I liked hanging out with you, too."

She was leading the way. When they turned right on Fisher, he thought he knew where they were going.

"I heard about what happened with you and Rick yesterday."

He just shrugged.

"I wanted to call you last night, but my dad was in one of his moods again."

"Sorry," was all he could think of to say. He wanted to ask her what happened when her dad got into these moods, but he was sure she wouldn't tell him. Besides, he wasn't sure if he wanted to know.

"You get around it."

Callum was aware of the evening air, the slight sweet scent of lilac trees, the smell of Cindy's hair, and the touch of her hand in his. He hoped his palm wouldn't start to sweat.

"They found out it wasn't you who wrecked his tires, right?"

Callum nodded.

"Does Rick believe it?" she went on.

"Yeah, I think he does. We had a little chat afterward."

"He didn't push you around anymore, did he?"

Callum smiled and looked down at her. "We just talked."

"About what?"

He wanted to tell her that they talked about her, that he knew why Rick was so protective of her. He decided it was best to leave the entire subject alone.

"Football," he said, grinning.

"You're kidding, right?"

He laughed. They were in Fisher Park now, near the low rows of bushes and thick trees known for their magical make-out properties. She grabbed him by the hands and pulled him into the trees to a little patch completely hidden from the path.

"You want to kiss me?"

He nodded, his heart pounding. He was sure his palms were sweating now.

"Well? What are you waiting for?"

He leaned forward, wondering which way to tilt his head, how much to tilt his nose out of the way, whether to open his mouth or keep it closed. All this and more flashed through his head in the instant it took to lower his head and kiss her. Their lips touched for a moment and Cindy opened her mouth slightly, and suddenly there was nothing at all in Callum's mind. After a little while they stopped and she looked up at him, smiling.

"Nice," she said.

He nodded, agreeing. They were standing very

close but not touching, except for holding hands.

"A hug would be nice," she added.

He stepped a little closer and put his arms around her, running one hand along her back. Cindy did the same. Just as he touched a spot below her shoulder blade, she touched one of the bruises along his ribs. They both winced and stepped back, dropping their arms.

"Sorry," Callum said

"Me, too," Cindy replied.

"I guess we're both accident-prone, huh?"

Callum nodded and smiled.

"I suppose," he said.

She moved in again and took his hands, placing them on her hips. "Let's try it again. I promise I won't hurt you this time."

"Okay," Callum replied. "And I promise not to hurt you."

"You better not," she said.

They kissed again, then stopped suddenly when they heard others crashing through the bushes, giggling. Before they could move apart, four other kids rushed into their little hiding spot. Callum was surprised to see Aidan and Tyler with their arms around Brandie and Sarah, respectively.

For a moment, no one spoke, they just stared at each other. As Tyler took in the sight, the grin left his face. He looked at Cindy, then at Callum, and his eyes went cold. Callum wondered how Tyler could hold a grudge, considering his arm was around another girl.

"What's going on here?" Sarah asked, laughing at the crazy situation they found themselves in.

"I was going to ask you that," Cindy said. She slipped to Callum's side and put her arm around his waist in a proprietary move. Callum slipped his arm over her shoulder, knowing it was expected of him.

"Nothing," Aidan said. "We were just hanging out."

"Looks like all of you are getting along great since Saturday," Cindy said.

"So are you two," Sarah said. She put her arm around Tyler and pulled him closer, but he just looked uncomfortable. Callum could hear a siren wailing in the distance, crickets chirp, feel the mosquitoes that had finally found them.

"Are we interrupting your walk or something?" Callum asked to break the silence.

The others looked at each other, grinning. Only Tyler didn't look happy.

"Actually, this is where we were headed," Aidan said.

"You can join us," Sarah said.

Callum looked at Cindy and knew that the moment they were having was now lost.

"It's a little crowded here," Cindy said. "Callum and I are going to head home."

"Suit yourself," Sarah replied.

Before they could get through the brush that separated their hiding spot from the path, the other four had started making out. Callum glanced back and caught a glimpse of Tyler staring at him.

It was almost dark when they stopped a few houses from Cindy's. She took him by the hand and pulled him into the shadows between two garages. She kissed him again, both of them being careful of each other's tender areas. After a while, she broke away, glancing at her watch.

"I better get home," Cindy said. "You stay here though, in case my dad's still outside."

Callum nodded. After all that kissing, walking would have been a bit awkward anyway. He wanted to make sure she knew that he wanted to see her again.

"Hey, Cindy!"

She stopped to look at him, waiting.

"Listen, we — my parents and me — are having a ceilidh on Saturday. Want to come? Aidan and Tyler are going to be there," he added quickly, as if somehow that would make it seem more appealing. He hadn't even thought about the party until now.

"A kay-lay?" she asked, confused and a little amused. "What is a kay-lay?"

"A party, with music and stuff."

She grinned. "Are you asking me out?"

"Well, no. I mean I want you to come to the party. I guess. Yes."

Callum could have kicked himself, he sounded like a fool, all that havering and talking stupid.

She ran a hand through her hair and grinned, acting if she was deep in thought.

"Okay. I guess. Yes," She mimicked his stammering. "If my dad lets me."

Callum nodded. He wondered what exactly she could do without his permission.

"Let's meet up tomorrow and walk to school, okay?" she said as she turned away.

"Sure," he replied. Callum stayed in the shadows until he could no longer see her.

Chapter 10

Callum waited at the corner for Cindy for nearly ten minutes. He looked at his watch, wondering why she was late and how much longer he dared stay before he would be late for school. For a moment he felt a deep dread, wondering if her father had been in "one of his moods" again when she got home from their work. Finally, he saw her walk down the lane, her backpack slung casually over her shoulder. He smiled and stood up straight, relieved and excited to see her at last. Then he saw she wasn't alone. Sarah and another girl were walking with her. Cindy waved from across the street.

"What's going on?" he asked her, quickly up to them.

"Oh, hey, Callum," Cindy said. "Can you go on ahead? We girls have to talk."

Callum stared at her, confused and beginning to

get angry. What was she doing? What game was she playing with him?

"I thought we …"

"Sorry. We just have to talk — you know, girl stuff. See you later."

They went on ahead, and he saw them giggling, Sarah looking over her shoulder at him.

Hurt and embarrassed, he crossed the street without looking back.

At school things got even weirder for Callum. He met up with Tyler and Aidan at the main entrance and walked in with them. Aidan was his usual talkative self, going on about last night, wanting details about what had happened with Cindy. Tyler was even less interested than usual, looking sullen as they walked down the hall to their lockers. Callum told them about what had happened this morning, how Cindy had completely ignored him.

Aidan just shrugged. "Chicks, man. What're you going to do?"

"Yeah," Tyler added. "Sucks to be you, doesn't it?"

Callum and Aidan both looked at him, surprised at his aggressive tone. Callum was already annoyed by Cindy's behaviour. Tyler's attitude just got on his nerves.

"What's your problem, anyway? Have I pissed you off or something?"

They had been friends for months now, but Callum wasn't going to ignore Tyler's attitude any longer. Just then, Aidan put his hand on Callum's shoulder and nodded at something behind Callum's back. Callum turned, and his heart skipped a beat when he saw Rick and his entourage heading down the hall toward them. The younger boys moved as close to their lockers as possible, hoping to somehow melt into the background. As the larger boys approached, one of them reached out as if to grab Callum. Rick grabbed him by the shoulder.

"Leave it," he said.

His friend stepped back and looked back at Rick. "What's your problem?"

"Nothing," Rick replied. "Just leave it."

With a final feint at Callum, the football player joined Rick and the others.

"What the hell just happened?" Aidan asked. Callum shook his head, a little stunned himself. Tyler turned away, shoving his books in his locker, then slamming it shut. He spun the dial on the lock and looked at Aidan.

"It's obvious, isn't it?" Tyler said as he pushed past Callum, deliberately hitting him with his shoulder. "Everyone's all in love with the immigrant." Aidan and Callum just stood there, surprised once more.

***

Callum sat in the bamboo room, looking at the school blogger's website. It seemed that Callum was the target again. There was a little article about Scottish men's affinity for sheep and wearing skirts. The blogger had found a photo of Callum and had used a photo program to make it look like he was wearing a kilt, complete with high heels and fishnet stockings.

Callum wasn't amused.

There were pictures of Rick and some of his teammates manipulated to make them look like they were in an orgy. The unknown blogger was becoming more cruel than funny on the website.

Callum stood up, grabbing for his headphones, when his phone chirped. He checked the call display — it was Cindy. He hesitated before flipping the phone open on the fourth ring.

"Hello?"

"Hey, Scottie! What's up?"

"Nothing," he replied noncommittally.

"You look good in a dress. I'm jealous."

Callum sighed and sat on the edge of his bed, absent-mindedly rubbing his knee. "You saw that, huh?"

"The whole school probably has by now."

"Terrific." School was getting to be more fun as each day passed.

"Don't worry. Everyone knows it's just a joke."

"I'm not laughing."

"I know what will cheer you up. You wanna go to the park again?"

Callum shifted around on his bed, wearily rubbing his forehead, feeling the anger and embarrassment from that morning return.

"You sure you have time for me?"

"What? Are you still pissy because of this morning? I told you, we needed to talk. Like I said, girl stuff!"

Girl stuff, Callum thought.

"Look," she said. "You want to come with me or —"

There was a shout and a loud banging noise Callum could easily hear over the phone. "My dad's home early. I'll call you back."

She rang off and Callum put his phone down on the table beside his bed. He didn't like what he had heard. He lay back on the bed, running his hands through his hair, thinking.

Callum jumped of his bed and ran upstairs. The family were all sitting in the living room watching TV. His brother and father sat in their chairs, each drinking their one evening beer, while his mother and Vickie sat on the sofa sipping tea and watching the show.

"Da, Ewan, can I ask you a favour?" Callum called, standing in the entrance to the living room. They both looked at him.

"What's up, son?" his father asked.

"Can you just come here? The both of you."

They both put their bottles on the coffee table and followed him into the foyer. They crossed their arms and looked down at him, waiting.

"Can you walk with me down to Cindy's house?"

"What? Are you feart of a lassie all of a sudden?" Ewan asked, smirking.

"It's her Da I'm feart about."

"What's the matter? He got the shotgun out already?" his father asked.

"Would you listen to me?" Callum shouted, getting angry. He had no time for their jokes. "I think he hits her and her Ma! I think he might be hurting her right now."

The smiles disappeared from their faces and they looked at him with concern.

"What makes you think so?"

"Stuff she told me before. And when I was on the mobile with her, I could hear her Ma and Da yelling in the background before Cindy rang off."

"You're positive about this?" Ewan asked.

"Aye! And what if I'm wrong, what harm will it do to check?"

They hesitated only a moment. "Show us the house," his father said and opened the door.

Callum practically had to run to keep pace with his father and brother as they rushed down the road to Cindy's. They hesitated at the gate, listening. The house seemed quiet, peaceful. The tiny yard out front was as meticulous as ever, the plants and grass trimmed to perfection. It was hard to believe that any kind of violence could be happening behind the tidy façade.

His father turned to Callum. "Are you sure —"

His question was cut short when they heard a man yelling, swearing horribly at someone, followed by a loud crashing noise. The three of them opened the gate and ran up to the front door. Ewan rang the doorbell, holding it down when no one came to the door. His father started banging on the door. At last, it swung open and Cindy's father stood there. He was a mess, not the perfectly dressed gardener Callum had seen before. His hair was sticking out in all directions, his shirt was unbuttoned almost to the waist and pulled out of his pants. He was flushed and breathing heavily. Callum could smell the beer on his breath.

"What do you want?" Cindy's father yelled.

"We want to make sure your wife and daughter are all right," Ewan shouted back.

His furious look made Cindy's father recoil slightly.

"What's it to you? I don't know who the hell you are!"

"We're your neighbours," Ewan said. "I want to see your wife and daughter. I want you to show me they're okay!"

Callum could see the other man puzzle over what he had said. Ewan's accent wasn't normally thick, but his anger had made it nearly impenetrable.

"Who are you? I don't know you. I don't know any of you. What are you anyway? A bunch of foreigners?"

"You know me," Callum replied. "I saw you on the weekend, hitting Cindy."

The father looked at him. "I remember you. I

told you and those other boys to stay away from her, didn't I? So what if she gets a slap now and then. Maybe she won't end up pregnant!"

"You think its okay for a grown man to slap a young girl?" Callum's father asked, stepping closer to the other man. Cindy's father was taller and thicker, but he had been drinking and was a lot softer-looking than Mr. McDuff.

"How I raise my kid's no business of yours!" Cindy's father shouted. "Now get off my property before I call the cops!"

"Aye!" Ewan shouted back. "Why don't you call the cops? We'll wait here until they show up. In fact, let's all go in and use your phone."

This made Cindy's father shut up at last. A few people walking past had stopped to watch the scene. A car passing by had slowed almost to a halt. The next-door neighbours were standing on their porch. Rick was one of them.

"It's okay," a woman's voice said. Callum looked back to the doorway and saw a woman who looked like a much older version of Cindy. She wore jeans and a long-sleeved cardigan that looked too heavy for the warm September evening. She had her arms wrapped tightly across her chest.

"Please," the woman said, "could you just leave? My husband and I were having an argument, is all. Just please go. You're just embarrassing us in front of the neighbours."

Callum's father and Ewan looked at her, then at the husband.

119

"Are you sure?" Callum's father asked her.

"Yes. Please go!"

"If you're afraid, we can —" Ewan started.

"Just go!" the woman said, cutting Ewan off.

They all looked at Cindy's father again, not hiding their contempt. Reluctantly they turned away and walked down the path.

"But, Da!" Callum said. "You know he's hurting them!"

"There's nothing we can do if she asks us to leave. It might even get worse for her if we don't," Ewan explained. Callum's father watched them go, tight-lipped and seething. The small crowd starting to disperse now that the action was over.

"And stay away from my place! Goddamn foreigners! Coming here, stealing our jobs. Barely speaking the language. Why don't you all go back to wherever the hell you came from?"

Callum's father spun on his heel and started to rush back toward Cindy's father. Ewan grabbed him and held him. Callum could see it was a struggle.

"No, Da! It's us that'll get the jail, not him." Cindy's father had been smart enough to shut the door and lock it as Ewan barely restrained his father. Callum held his father by the arm and could feel the biceps bulging, the tension running through him. He had seen his father this angry only once before, and that was the day a year ago in spring when Callum had been attacked.

They walked out of the yard, not bothering to

shut the garden gate. As they turned back to their own home, Rick walked down his path to the sidewalk, looking nervous and worried. He glanced over at Cindy's house again as if he could see through the walls. Standing next to Callum's father and brother, Rick seemed much smaller.

"It'll quiet down now," Rick said. "It always gets bad just after he gets home from drinking. Once he knocks them around a bit, he calms down."

"You knew this all the time and didn't say anything?" Callum asked.

Rick rubbed his forehead and ran his hand across the back of his neck. Incredibly, he looked close to tears.

"It didn't get this bad until a couple of years ago. That's when the base closed and all the soldiers and jobs left. He hasn't worked since."

"He was a soldier?" Callum's father had always felt it was an honour to be a soldier, and that his duty was to protect the helpless.

"Rick nodded. My folks called the cops the first couple of times it got bad. They couldn't do anything. Cindy's mom defended him, saying they were just having an argument."

Callum's dad and brother just shook their heads. Callum looked over at the now-quiet house.

"After the cops came, it always got worse anyway," Rick said. "So we stopped calling them."

"What's your name?" Ewan asked. Callum

introduced them, simply telling them that Rick was a friend from school. He had never thought he would consider Rick a friend, but he was beginning to understand more about Rick's behaviour.

"If you see him hurting them, if you only suspect it, call us. Okay?" Ewan said.

"I guess," said Rick slowly. "But what are you going to do that the cops can't?"

"Next time he hurts them, there won't be a polite chat, I can tell you. And he'll need an ambulance, not the cops!" Callum's father told him.

Rick stopped Callum from following his father and brother back to their house.

"Hey! Thanks for trying to do something," he said awkwardly.

"Isn't there anything else we can do? Maybe talk to someone at school?"

Rick shrugged. "Like I said, unless Cindy or her mom tells the cops what he's doing, no one can do anything."

"What about Taggart?"

"The old cop at school? What can he do?"

"I don't know, but we could talk to him. Maybe he knows what to do."

Rick sighed. "I guess we could ask."

"Tomorrow at school. We'll go see him, okay?"

Rick hesitated. He glanced at Cindy's eerily quiet house. Callum knew that he was thinking of Cindy, alone in there with a monster.

"No," Rick said at last. "We have to wait."

"What? Why? He's going to keep hurting —"

Rick cut him off, shouting. "I know! I've known it for years now! I just want to be sure. I want to think it over, make sure we're not going to screw up her life even more."

Callum was stunned by this. How could waiting help?

"I read about this," Rick said, as if answering Callum's thoughts. "Things can get worse once the family gets separated. A lot worse. We have to think this out. A couple of days, okay?"

Callum sighed deeply, itching to do something right now, tonight. But Rick was older, so maybe he knew something Callum didn't. He nodded and ran up the block to catch up with his father and brother.

***

Callum couldn't sleep, thinking of that disgusting old man hitting Cindy and her mother, thinking how helpless he was to do anything. He sat at his desk and logged onto the Internet, linking to the school's blogger out of habit. He was angry and shocked to see that there was a new link. Callum opened it and saw little lines of text scroll along the bottom of the screen.

Fellow student gets a bit of what for from her dad, and our Scottish "Bravehearts" come to the rescue — kinda!

The familiar shaky camera was positioned outside Cindy's house, showing the entire confrontation that had taken place only a couple of hours before.

The caption underneath went on:

Give the Bravehearts E for effort — but guess how the old domestics usually end up (statistically speaking).

The video ended with a disgusting photo of a young girl lying in a morgue, her body opened for an autopsy.

Callum wanted to pick up his laptop and smash it against the basement wall. Instead he slammed it shut and paced his bamboo room. Who was this blogger? And why did he seem to be targeting Callum and his friends?

How did he always seem to know where to be?

Chapter 11

Once more, Aidan, Tyler, and Callum were walking to school. No one discussed what had happened the night before. Callum had shut down his friends quickly when they had tried. Aidan tried to change the topic — a little. "Hey, Cal, you and your family starred on the blogger's website last night! Tyler, did you see?"

Callum looked daggers at Aidan. Tyler just looked bored. "I didn't look at the blog last night, and I'm glad now. Who wants to hear more about Callum?"

There was only one good thing about going to school that morning: Callum knew that the bullying was over, at least for the time being.

They were reaching the end of the alley when Tyler shifted his backpack from one shoulder to the other. As he did, his jacket lifted up. Aidan and Callum caught sight of something glinting in the morning sun.

"What have you got there?" Aidan asked, reaching for the metallic object wedged in the waist of Tyler's jeans.

"What?" Tyler looked defensive. Aidan reached out to grab the object.

"Leave it!" Tyler shouted, trying to twist away. He was too slow, and Aidan had it. All those hours in front of a computer hadn't left Tyler very fit. Aidan held it so Callum could get a better look. It was a large military-style knife with a heavy, thick blade, razor sharp on one side, with ugly serrated teeth on the other. Callum felt himself shiver at the sight of the steel shining in the sunlight.

"Where'd you get this?" Aidan asked Tyler. He was smiling as he held it up, turning it slowly. He was appreciating the weight of it, the power it seemed to exude.

Callum hated the sight of it.

"Give it back, okay?" Tyler said, almost pleading.

"Just tell me where you got it."

"I bought it online, at this surplus site from the States. Give it back!" He was reaching for it, trying to snatch it out of Aidan's hand, but Aidan easily kept it out of his reach.

"It's pretty cool," Aidan said. "Why did you bring it to school?"

"Why do you think? For protection."

"Against what? Ninjas?" Aidan asked, laughing.

"No! That asshole Rick and his friends."

Callum looked at the knife nervously. "They've barely bothered you this year."

"You never know what'll happen. Or who to trust."

"Put it away," Callum said quietly.

Aidan saw something in Callum's face and his smile faded. He lifted the sheath and slid the ugly killing thing into it. Tyler snatched it out of his hands.

"What's the matter, Cal?" Tyler asked. "Scared you'll get hurt?"

"Just put the damn thing away!" Callum shouted.

"Don't worry," Tyler said, sliding the knife out of the sheath. "I know how to handle it. I've been practising."

He fell into crouch, waving the knife back and forth menacingly. He started to circle around his friends, tossing the knife back and forth between hands. He looked almost comical, his slightly pudgy body moving ungracefully, imitating moves from some bad movie.

Aidan just laughed at him. "Man, you've got way too much free time!"

He didn't seem to notice the strange glint in Tyler's eye, the feeling of power the knife so obviously lent him.

"The Marines tell you to go for the throat. Or if you cut the back of the knee and slice the tendons, that disables them."

Callum felt the pain as Tyler's words sank in.

He could feel the deep pain run along the muscles of his calf, the deep itch inside the scar that never seemed to fade with time.

"Hey, guys," Aidan said softly, looking back and forth between Callum and Tyler. "Let's take it easy, okay?"

Tyler kept circling Callum, letting the blade shine in the sun, twisting it around in a stylized way. Without having to look, without taking his eyes off his opponent — the way his father had taught him — Callum knew that a crowd was gathering, curious students on their way to school stopping to see the impromptu entertainment. He realized that he had crouched into a defensive position, his feet flat on the ground, his body ready. That was why his knee had flared up, why he could feel the grinding of tendon and bone as he moved around, mirroring Tyler's actions.

"You go for the jugular, not across the throat, 'cause that might not kill right away." Tyler continued in a voice that contained his emotions.

"All right, Tyler! Enough!" Aidan shouted. "You too, Cal. This isn't a game."

Callum heard him as if at a distance. He could feel sweat run down his back, feel more sweat along his leg as the strain pushed it to the limit. He became aware of his heart beating in his chest, pounding and pounding from a mix of fear and a strange excitement.

"You go for the liver as well," Tyler continued his chant of violence, ignoring Aidan. "It takes a bit longer, but you nick the liver and they bleed out, guaranteed."

"Put it away," Callum said softly, almost in a whisper. "This is your last chance."

"What's the matter, Braveheart? I thought all you Scotch guys carried knives?"

"What'd you call me?" One word set off connections in Callum's brain, even through the concentration he focused on Tyler and the knife.

"What?" Tyler replied. "Nothing. I just said all you —"

"You called me Braveheart."

"Yeah? So? It was a movie, remember? Besides, that's what you were called on the blog."

"But you said you didn't read it," Aidan said.

"I didn't," Tyler replied, his concentration broken at mention of the blog. He was still circling, but he didn't look menacing anymore. He looked like a young boy playing a silly war game.

"Then how did you know about the Braveheart thing?" Callum asked.

"Look, this is stupid! Maybe I did see it, okay? I don't remember. What's the big deal anyway?"

He looked nervous now, his face pale and the glee he had shown while brandishing the knife gone. He still held the knife pointed at Callum, but he was slowing.

"It's you, isn't it? Callum shouted, the realization coming to him all at once. "It's your blog!"

"No way!" Tyler replied. "I … I mean … Why would I?"

"It makes sense," Aidan added. "That's why the blogger always was around when stuff happened to us. Like when Cal was tossed by Rick, or when we threw the soap in the fountain."

"This is crazy! You're my friends!"

"Are we? Are we really your friends? Am I your friend?"

Callum stepped closer to Tyler. He was angry, but not angry enough to stop being wary of the knife. Tyler was close to tears. When he noticed how close Callum was, Tyler waved the knife in an arc and inched away from him. He slashed at the space between them.

Callum stepped forward and grabbed Tyler's knife hand, tossing him off-balance and onto the ground. He stepped over Tyler, twisting the arm until Tyler screamed in pain and dropped the knife.

"Don't you ever point a knife at me, ya nyaff!"

Callum still held the arm, still twisted it back, his anger so huge that he wanted to keep twisting until he felt something snap.

"Callum!" a girl shouted. "Leave him alone!" It was Sarah. She looked frightened.

"Why'd you have to move here?" Tyler shouted at Callum through his tears of pain and embarrassment. "Things were great before you! And Cindy would be going out with me!"

Sarah grew pale as Tyler's words sunk in. Tyler seemed to notice her for the first time.

"Wait! Sarah!" he shouted as she turned away and pushed through the crowd. "I didn't mean ..."

He shut up, seeing that she was gone.

Tyler started to twist again, still held to the ground by Callum's grip. Callum was sweating even more from the morning heat, the adrenaline, and the pain from his shattered leg. His anger was intense. All he could think about was the knife in front of him, all the other knives he could barely recall from last year.

"Is that what this is about?" Callum said. "You think Cindy would actually be interested in some flabby piece of shyte like you?"

"This happened before Cindy and Callum got together," Aidan pointed out. "You were blogging the first day of school."

"Everybody thought Callum was so cool! All the kids, even the teachers. Just because he's foreign has that stupid accent! Even Rick loves you now!"

Callum was still holding the arm, twisting it, making Tyler's face press into the grass beside the alley. A part of him understood how he might feel if some new kid seemed to walk in and take over, how even the bullies who had terrorized him for years seemed to be won over. He could understand it, but he was far from ready to forgive.

Aidan touched his arm. "Dude, let him go. You're hurting him."

"That's the idea."

"He's our friend."

"He never was my friend. He's hated me the whole time."

Callum swallowed hard, feeling tears rise. He released Tyler's arm and stepped away.

"Get out of my sight!" he said.

Tyler got up on his knees warily, rubbing his shoulder. As he reached for his backpack, he grabbed the knife off the ground. He swung back-handed along Callum's leg, the blade slicing through Callum's jeans as though they were tissue, the blade sliding over his leg just below his knee. His bad knee.

Callum howled in pain and Aidan stepped forward, kicking Tyler in the chest. Tyler fell back, winded, then jumped up quickly, still holding out the knife. He backed away from the others. The crowd moved out of his way as he spun around and ran, not toward school, but in the direction of his house.

Callum lay on the ground holding his knee, not noticing the blood spilling through his tightly clasped fingers. He rocked back and forth, breathing in quick bursts, trying to calm himself, trying to make the pain subside.

"Dude!" Aidan shouted as he crouched down beside him. "Cal! Oh, Jesus Christ! What the hell's happening?"

Aidan shouted at the gaping crowd to get lost. Then he turned back to Callum. "Let me see."

Callum reluctantly let go of his knee and the pain exploded again, making fresh tears pool in his eyes. He lay back on the cool grass and stared at the sky, wiping the new blood on his hands onto the grass. He felt Aidan open the torn leg of his pant.

"I don't think it's deep, he said. "But you're going to need stitch — Holy crap!"

Aidan's face had gone pale.

"Cal," he said. "I always knew what happened … But, Jesus!"

Aidan had seen the scars, the damage left over from last spring.

"No wonder you never wore shorts," Aidan continued.

Callum sat up, ignoring him. The pain was still there, but it was fading. He grabbed his backpack, tore it open, and pulled out his gym T-shirt and a bottle of water. He poured the water over the wound and held the shirt to it. Blood blossomed on it. He took a deep breath and wiped the tears from his eyes, attempting what he hoped was a smile.

"What do you say to skipping school and getting me sewn up somewhere?"

Chapter 12

Callum pushed through the crowd toward Cindy, Aidan, and Brandie. He carried drinks for all of them, ice cold on a small tray that his father had picked up from his favourite pub back in Glasgow. The three of them stood at the edge of the patio, bewildered by the sight of all the people milling around in Ewan's small backyard. Callum was glad that no one seemed to notice that he was walking with a more pronounced limp than usual as he picked his way through the party.

After the incident Monday morning, Aidan used his debit card to get a cab to take Callum to the nearest clinic. Aidan had also bought him a new pair of jeans, to Callum's everlasting gratitude. There was no way he could go home to his mother in torn and blood-splattered pants. He had thrown out his blood-stained T-shirt, and hoped he could slip the loss and the new jeans past his mother's eerily watchful eye. So far he had been successful on both counts.

Callum handed his friends the deep bronze-coloured drink from the round bar tray. Aidan grabbed his first glass, pulling a small bottle from his pocket with the other hand.

"Want to spice it up?" he whispered to the others.

Aidan held a tiny bottle of whiskey, the kind Callum had seen on the airplane flying from Scotland. While Callum made sure his parents weren't looking, Aidan ripped off the cap and poured a little whiskey into each of the glasses. They held up their now-potent drinks in a salute.

"How do you say 'cheers' in Scotland?" Brandie asked.

"Slainte!" Callum exclaimed proudly.

"Schlong?" Cindy asked, and they all laughed. Callum was about to correct her, but left it alone. He was just happy she was happy. It had taken him a long time to convince her to come to the party after the scene at her place.

"Here's to schlongs!" Aidan said and they all took a long sip. Then, simultaneously, they all spat out the concoction!

"Jesus!" Aidan exclaimed. "What the hell is this?"

Callum was trying to get the taste out of his mouth. The combination of the whisky and the sweet soft drink was sickening.

"It's the booze," he said at last.

"No it isn't," Brandie said. "It's this drink. What is it?"

Callum was a little deflated. He had served them his favourite beverage, Irn Bru, perhaps Scotland's second national drink after whiskey.

"What flavour is it supposed to be?" Cindy asked.

Callum was stumped. He had no idea what flavour it was supposed to be. It was just Irn Bru!

"Does your brother have any cranberry juice?" she asked as she put her glass back on the tray.

"Way to waste good booze, Dude," Aidan said as he and the girls walked past Callum toward the house. Callum emptied their glasses one at a time into the flower bed along the fence, hoping it wouldn't stop the dying plants from growing next year.

"Way to waste good Irn Bru," he said softly to himself.

A few minutes later they were gathered together again, watching the adults. Ewan was playing a Shooglnifty CD loudly over his brand-new stereo, bought specially for the occasion. The bright Celtic melodies were making a few of the adults swivel their hips in time. Ewan and his father both wore kilts and blue T-shirts with the red-and-yellow lion rampant of Scotland emblazoned on the front.

"You dad and brother look pretty hot in that outfit," Cindy said, nudging Callum in the ribs gently.

"Yeah," Brandie said. "Who knew a guy could look good in a skirt?"

"Brandie," Cindy said, giggling, "go home and get a couple of your uniform kilts. Let's see what the boys look like!"

Aidan caught Callum's eye — the girls were kidding, weren't they? Callum hurried to tell them that, since the movie *Braveheart* had come out, there was a rebirth in Scotland's pride in its heritage. Kilts and Gaelic and all things Scottish were trendy again. People who had never been anywhere near the highlands now sported kilts, and a few rock stars had even tried to make them the new fashion.

Ewan and Vickie were mingling with their guests, most of them Canadian, but a few Scots that Ewan and their parents had met over the last few months. Callum's father was standing by the barbecue, trying to get his wife to dance to the music. She just laughed and pushed him away, turning back to talk to another woman. Still dancing, the pleats of his kilt swaying as he moved, he attended the food: steaks, hamburgers, and marinated chicken. Thick slices of haggis and blood sausage were steaming over the flames, wrapped in little foil packets to add a surprise Scottish flavour to the meal.

"Time to eat!" his father shouted to the crowd.

***

None of Callum's friends tried any of the Scottish delicacies. He tried to convince them that it was actually good but after their experience with Irn Bru, they just shouted him down and dug into the burgers and chicken.

The fall sun was fading and the night cooling after the meal was eaten. Ewan and his father wandered around topping up drinks while Ma took away dishes and Vickie turned on the propane patio heaters they had rented for the evening. The CD changed and the sound of folk-singer Dougie Maclean singing "Scots Wa Hae" wafted on the cool air.

Callum tried to slide behind his friends, knowing what was coming. His father looked frantically around, putting his beer on a nearby table.

"Where are they?" he yelled. "Where's my wee partners?"

Ever since Callum was young, McDuff father and sons would sing that song together. But Callum had no interest in singing it in front of Cindy and the others.

"Come on, the pair of you!"

Vickie caught Callum trying to hide and dragged him over to the barbecue.

"This I have to hear," she shouted as she pulled Callum through the crowd. Ewan was already there, ready to sing.

"Start the song again," his father shouted and Vickie scanned the CD back. Callum sang along quietly, embarrassed and worried what Cindy would think of it all. As the song progressed, his mind turned to the song lyrics he was singing, words that suddenly had new meaning for him. Something stirred inside him, and he began to understand why this particular song held so much meaning for his father. They sang it together, and to Callum's ear, not at all badly.

Lay the proud usurper low …
Tyrants fall and every foe …
Liberty's in every blow
Let us do or die!

As the song ended, there was a tremendous burst of applause and all three McDuff men took a deep bow. Callum's father finished it off with a deep curtsy, fanning the skirts of his kilt wide. Callum slid out of the spotlight and back to his friends, who seemed impressed rather than embarrassed for him.

"Where's that Irish bassa Gallagher?" Callum winced as his father's voice cut through the chatter. Aidan went a little pale. His parents were at the party and, even though it had been a few generations since they had lived in Ireland, they still loved the old songs. Aidan's father made his way across the yard and joined Callum's by the barbecue. He was shorter than Callum's dad, with thick reddish hair and a broad face. The two men clinked bottles together before they sang a rendition of "When Irish Eyes are Smiling." Surprisingly, both men had decent voices and they sang well together.

"Aidan!" his father yelled. "Get up here and give us a song."

Aidan hardly hesitated. What would be the point? He drew Brandie close, an arm around her waist, kissed her as if he were an old-fashioned swashbuckler off to war, and ran to the barbecue area. Ever the clown, he decided to play it for laughs. He sang a song Callum had never heard before, a silly Irish-sounding song about a baby being thrown out with her bathwater. Aidan sang with all his might in a thick fake accent.

And me mother got drunk
And me father was drunk
And me grandma spat in his eye,
And some think it a laugh
To be tossed with the bath
But as for meself —
I'll stay dry!

He ran off to applause. He rejoined their little group and, this time, Brandie kissed him. Cindy looked up at Callum and slipped her hand in his, resting her head against his shoulder. More people got up to sing a song, some more successfully than others. Someone had brought a tin flute, another a harmonica. As the shadows deepened and the flames from the torches got darker, the songs became more dark, more sorrowful.

Callum's mother took a sip of her gin and tonic and stood. Callum saw the look on his father's face as he glanced over to catch his son's eye. It was the first time Callum's mother had offered to sing in a long time, although he had caught her singing softly to herself as she busied herself around the house. She sang in a sweet, nearly professional voice and he felt tears sting as he realized how much he had missed her singing.

Where are you now my Bonnie Eilean,
Yearning for bairns torn unweaned
Then scattered to the winds
Seeking for rest
And to come home at last
To your loving breast.

Callum could sense the mood change as she sang the mournful tune, Celtic hearts yearning for the country they had left behind. He felt it as well, the pull of his native soil, along with a deep pang of guilt for being the cause of his family's departure.

***

They stood together in the deep shadows of the trees in Fisher Park, alone, except for Aidan and Brandie off somewhere in their own hiding place. Cindy was kissing Callum deeply. Then she looked up into his eyes.

"I had fun tonight," she said at last.

"Me too. I'm having more fun now." He leaned down to kiss her again. After a while, she stopped to speak again.

"It's too bad you didn't wear a kilt."

"You wouldn't think so if you'd seen my legs," he replied.

"Maybe I want to see your legs."

He grinned and kissed her along her throat. "Maybe I want to see yours."

"If you were wearing a kilt, I could run my hands up along your legs and underneath …" she said, a sultry look in her eye. And as she spoke, hands moved up his legs.

"I guess you'll have to use your imagination then," Callum said as his heart beat faster and faster.

"I already am," Cindy replied as she pulled him down to the grass, which was already turning brown, ready for winter.

***

Callum and Cindy walked hand in hand down the street. The breeze was blowing elm leaves around, but neither paid the slightest attention to anything but each other. Callum felt his heart sink a little as they came to her house, standing across the street from it in the shadows.

"I guess I better get going," Cindy said. They stood there, looking at the house.

He didn't want to let her go, didn't want the evening to end. Mostly, he didn't want her to go inside those walls, vulnerable to whatever lay behind that door.

"Do you have to go?" he asked.

"I have to go home sometime," she said, laughing.

"I know. I just wish …"

"Wish what?" Her smile faded a little.

"It's just that it's not safe. Your dad …"

"What about my dad?" she asked him, suddenly looking annoyed. "Look, I told you and I told Rick. Don't worry about me. I can take care of myself. It's *my* home, right?"

He nodded his head, agreeing with her, not wanting her to be angry with him — not understanding why she was angry.

"I'll see you later, okay?" she said, giving him a quick kiss.

"Can we do something tomorrow?"

"We'll see," she said and waved as she ran across the street and up her path to the front door. She slipped inside without bothering to look back at him. As he turned to walk away, the lights snapping on in the house caught at the corner of his eye. He felt a coldness inside and wanted to walk right up, to knock on the door and demand to see that she was okay. He sighed and knew that he couldn't. He would talk to Rick on Monday. Even if Rick wasn't ready yet, they would meet with Taggart.

Chapter 13

Rick and Callum sat across the desk from Constable Taggart as he lowered himself into his chair. Slowly he took a notebook from his desk drawer and laid it down on the blotter. Then he took a pencil from a small tray on the desk and laid it on the pad. He sat back in his chair, arms crossed over his uniformed chest, and stared at the boys.

When they had asked to meet him, he had agreed right away, no doubt thinking it was about Rick's car. As they walked to his office, Callum wondered again where Cindy was hiding. She had not called him; when he walked past her house, there was no sign of life.

"So," Taggart said at last. "What has caused this momentous occasion?"

Rick and Callum looked at each other, and Rick nodded for him to start.

"Well," Callum stated, choosing his words

carefully. What if we knew someone was hurting someone else? What could we do about it?"

"Is this happening at school?"

Callum shook his head.

"Is Mr. Atkins, here, involved?"

Callum looked at Rick, saw him flush slightly.

"No. Neither of us are involved. It's a girl here at school. A friend of ours."

"Who's hurting her? A boyfriend?"

Taggart had uncrossed his arms and picked up the pencil, to take notes.

Callum sighed and started to tell Taggart everything he knew. Rick added more information, including the fact that it had started when Cindy's father retired from the army, and how it had escalated since then. Taggart said little and continued making notes.

"What's the girl's name?" he asked when they had finished their story.

The boys looked at each other.

"She's all embarrassed about this," Rick said. "She'll hate us if she knew we told you."

"Wait," Taggart said, holding out a hand. He reached over to the filing cabinet stuck next to the desk in his tiny office. He pulled out a file and opened it on the blotter.

"Cindy Holland," he said out loud, reading from the top page of the file. "She lives at 429 Morley Avenue. Currently in grade nine at this school."

Rick and Callum looked at each other in

amazement as Taggart explained. "We have been aware of Cindy's situation for some time. There have been police reports, as well as those from the guidance counsellor."

"Then why haven't you done anything?" Callum shouted.

"Have you any reason to believe she couldn't make it to class because her father hurt her?"

"Who knows?" Rick replied. "He never seems to hurt them bad enough that they can't go to school or to work the next day. And I hardly ever see any marks on Cindy any more."

Callum thought of the long-sleeved shirts Cindy always wore, the way she had flinched in pain the first time he hugged her.

"Have either of you actually witnessed any abuse?"

Callum could only tell him of the time her father had hit Cindy when they returned home from the mall. Rick had a few more stories to tell.

"All right," Taggart said at last. "Now, I have to tell you something. And I need you to know I am telling you this in confidence. None of it leaves this room. Understand?

When the two boys nodded their promise to keep quiet, he continued. "Yesterday, the police arrested Cindy's father. He put his wife in hospital this time."

"Where's Cindy?" Callum and Rick spoke at the same time. Rick rose from his seat.

"She's fine," Taggart assured him. "She's with

a relative nearby." He slid two pieces of paper across his desk to the two boys. "Look, we may need you to testify," he said. "I need you to write down what you've seen. And then date and sign your statement at the bottom. There's no guarantee that Cindy's mother will testify against her husband."

"Even after this?" Rick asked, obviously confused by such behaviour. Callum understood it — all too well. He knew the sick feeling inside when the fear overtakes you and you'd rather face the pain than the fear.

***

Callum lay on his bed, his completed homework tossed on the floor. Once more, trying to focus on the music throbbing through his headphones. It was strange how important music had become to him, how much a part of his life it was. Before he was attacked, the only thing that really mattered was football. He lived and breathed for the game, and practised on his own for hours even after a long day practising with his team. During the long recovery period from the attack, he had listened to music, anything he could get hold of. It had helped take his mind off all the surgeries, the endless hours of therapy it took to get him walking again.

Now he was trying to listen to the CD, but all he could think about was Cindy. Days had passed since he and Rick had spoken with Taggart, and neither had seen or heard from her.

He was about to shut off the CD and get another one — something he could concentrate on, maybe an old Alex Harvey or Pixies CD — when his phone rang. It was Cindy's ringtone. He scrambled to pull off the headphones and sit up, fumbling open the phone.

"Hello?" he almost shouted, heart racing.

"We need to talk," Cindy said. Even over the phone he could hear the coldness in her tone.

"When?"

"Now. I'll meet you and Rick at Fisher Park in fifteen."

***

It took less than ten minutes for Callum to throw track pants on over the tartan shorts he wore as pyjamas, pull on his hoodie, and get to Fisher Park. Rick was there already, looking extremely nervous. It was hard to believe that only a few weeks ago, just the sight of Rick terrified Callum. Now he saw Rick as just another zit-faced kid, bigger than most, trying to figure it all out.

"What you think she wants?" Rick asked as Callum joined him.

"Probably to tell us off for interfering in her life," Callum replied.

They sat on a bench and waited. Callum could feel coolness in the air, a strong hint of the famous

Winnipeg winter he had heard so much about. He saw that leaves on most of the trees were already falling.

After about ten minutes of silence, Cindy finally arrived. Her arms were crossed over her chest. She looked cold and angry.

"Let's walk," she said as she passed the bench they sat on. Both boys jumped up to follow her. They were deep into the park before she spun around.

"How are you guys?" she asked, a cold smile touching the edges of her mouth.

"Okay," both of them managed to sputter.

"Great. You wanna know how I'm doing?"

Before the boys could figure out who would answer, or how to answer, she pushed on.

"Oh wait! I forgot. You already know, don't you? It seems you two know everything about my life! Right?" She was angry, angrier than Callum had ever seen her.

"You know what's been going on since you talked to Taggart?" she shouted. "Since both of you felt you could rat me out to the school cop?"

"Cindy," Rick began. "We wanted to help, that's all!"

"Well, you sure helped all right!"

She pushed Rick, then Callum. Hard.

"You want to know how my life is ruined because you two couldn't keep your mouths shut?"

Both boys kept quiet and let her yell.

"Well, let's see. My dad's been arrested and locked up. My mother's been transferred to the nutjob ward because she had some kind of breakdown. And me? I'm staying at my aunt's because I can't go home!"

She pushed them again, and they saw she was close to tears.

"It's going to get better now," Rick said. "Now your dad's gone. Your mom will get better, too, and you can go home."

"Oh yeah? And I guess we'll all live happily ever after, right?"

She stared up and yelled into his face. "So what happens when Dad gets out of jail in a couple more days? You think he's going to forget that the little wife turned him in and tore his family apart?"

She jabbed him in the chest with her finger, then turned to Callum.

"How forgiving would you be if you got pulled out of your own house in handcuffs in front of the whole neighbourhood?"

Callum opened his mouth, but nothing came out.

"We can help you now, Cindy," Rick said.

"We won't let him touch either of you ever again," Callum added.

"Oh, so you two are going to move in with us? Are we all going to share a bed, too? Is that what you think?"

She started to cry, covering her face and pushing past them down the path. Rick and Callum went after her. Rick grabbed her, holding her by the arms while she kicked and screamed and swore at him.

"We can help," Rick said. "We'll think of something!"

Callum wished he could be as positive as Rick. But all he could do was stand there, letting Cindy's pain and anger wash over him.

Chapter 14

Cindy wouldn't listen — she kept struggling and screaming at Rick to let her go. Callum started to move in closer when someone pushed past him and ran into Rick, hitting him low, knocking the wind out of him.

The figure rushed at him again and Rick, trying to hold on to Cindy, went down on his back. The other boy jumped on his chest, punching him wildly.

"Leave her alone, you bastard!"

Tyler's voice was like Callum's cue to move, to do something. He rushed forward and grabbed Tyler under the armpits. Tyler's elbows smacked against the side of Callum's head as he lifted him up from on top of Rick and tossed him to the ground.

"Calm down, Tyler!" Callum shouted. "It's not what you think!"

Tyler was in hysterics. He was screaming as Rick stood and lurched over to Tyler.

Callum got between them.

"No!" he shouted at Rick, holding him back. "He just wants to protect Cindy."

Rick was angry, and he was ready to take that anger out on Tyler. Callum knew he couldn't hold him much longer.

"Were you following me again, you little creep?" Cindy shouted at Tyler.

"Someone has to look after you," Tyler said. He turned to Callum who was managing to hold Rick back. "I don't need your help," Tyler shouted as he jumped to his feet and pulled something from the waist of his jeans.

Rick finally pushed Callum aside and made a rush at Tyler. He stopped dead when he saw what was in Tyler's hand.

Tyler was crouched low, grinning in the fading light. In his right hand he held the ugly knife, waving it slowly back and forth in front of Rick.

"So, what does little Tyler have there?" Rick asked, anger edging the amusement in his voice.

"This is payback. For all the wedgies and charley-horses, all the times you slapped us around, tripped us up. All the times you made us look like idiots just because you're bigger." Tyler indicated the knife in his hand. "This makes us equal."

Rick was circling, looking for his chance. He made a few feints at Tyler, and each time Tyler swung the knife, barely missing him. Callum could see that Rick thought it was an act, that Tyler didn't have the guts to actually use the knife. He knew that Rick was wrong.

"Stop it!" Cindy shouted, and stepped toward the arc of the knife's blade as he swung it at Rick. Callum jumped forward and grabbed her. Rick turned to see Callum pull her back to safety. Just then, Tyler slashed out. Rick screamed in pain. He held his arm near the wrist, and Callum saw the blood pouring from under his fingers.

"You son of a bitch!" Cindy yelled as she moved in again. Tyler ignored her and went after Rick, who stumbled backward before tripping on the root of a tree and crashing to the ground.

Callum felt a cold rage well up inside him as he tried to hold Cindy back and watched Tyler loom over Rick, the knife held high over his head.

"Enough!" Callum shouted. "All of you! Enough!"

A year of anger, fear, and frustration poured out of Callum. The three of them froze and stared at him.

"You think you're all so tough? You think all this is some game? None of you — not one — has a clue about what's happening here!"

He pulled his hoodie off over his head, then the T-shirt.

"Is this what you want to happen? Is this what will make you feel like big men?"

Under the light of the full moon and the lights

along the path, his scars glowed eerily, a silver roadmap of pain. Cindy's mouth formed an O of shock. Rick and Tyler seemed frozen by the sight of the thick scars that ran along Callum's ribs and chest, the deep troughs they cut through his pale flesh. There were a few divots where the broken ribs had not healed properly.

"How's that?" Callum shouted. "Not enough? You want to see more?"

He slipped off his track pants and stood in front of them in his old tartan shorts. Cindy put her hand over her face and Callum saw her tears slipping through her fingers. It didn't matter to him. He still felt only coldness inside, only disgust at their little games. He saw them stare at his leg, where the damage was much worse than the scarring to his upper body. Callum's right leg looked thinner than his left. Huge scars criss-crossed it, from above the knee to the ankle. It looked as though chunks had been torn from the meat of his calf. Endless surgeries had left horrible ropy scars, and there were holes where pins and bars had been stapled to hold his shattered leg together.

"Jesus!" Tyler said at last. Callum rushed forward and grabbed the knife from him, tossing it as hard as he could. It arced in a slow circle and glinted once in the moonlight before falling somewhere on the road, clattering on the asphalt.

"You think you're a tough guy because you can use a knife? You're nothing but a pathetic little boy who lives his life in front of a video screen."

155

ealized that there were tears in his eyes as
urned to Rick, still holding his bleeding wrist,
aring up from the ground at Callum's feet.

"And you. Kidding yourself that you're really a
nice guy inside, always ready to stop your pals if
they get too tough on the little losers. But you
never had the guts to stop them in the first place.
Or to really help Cindy."

Finally Callum found himself to look at her.

"You might be the worst of all. Playing mind
games with us, playing us against each other.
Enjoying the power you have over all us stupid
males."

Callum was suddenly chilled. He could see his
breath in the cool evening and knew he had said
everything he needed to. He picked up his pants
and slipped them on, his back to the others. He
grabbed his shirt and hoodie. Then he walked
away.

He thought he heard Cindy call out to him as he
stepped onto the street. He ignored her, only stopping when he came across the knife. It looked like
Tyler hadn't got the deal he thought he had. The
knife lay on the ground, its cheap blade shattered.
Callum kicked it and the bits slid through a sewer
grate and away.

Chapter 15

The wean was laughing.

Callum gently kicked the old, scarred football to his four-year-old cousin Patrick. The little boy ran after it, slipping on the wet grass as he tried to kick it back. For a moment, Callum thought he was going to cry, but his little cousin jumped back on his feet and continued on, dribbling and trying to kick the ball past Callum.

They had been playing in the field behind the McDuff's small semi-detached house for half an hour, but Patrick was showing no signs of slowing down. Inside, Callum's mother and her sister were drinking tea and gossiping. His aunt lived in Barlanark, on the southeast part of Glasgow. Callum and his family lived in the Gorbells, once famous for being the roughest part of a rough city.

It was because his cousin was so happy, and because he had to watch him, that Callum didn't notice the three older boys until they were already walking across the field toward him.

The first rock barely missed the side of his head.

He turned to see where it had come from just as the next rock hit him high on the left side of his chest. He panicked then, even as he dodged the next couple of rocks thrown at him. His first instinct was to look around, to see if anyone had his back, if by some miracle his mates had chosen that moment to walk down the lane. No one was there. Then he checked his exits, ones he knew by heart — he had lived in the same house his whole life.

He had only one option.

"What do ye dae if there's mere than ain?" his Da had asked, time and time again.

"Run!" Callum replied.

"Exactly," his Da always said, grinning.

But Callum couldn't run. He couldn't run fast enough carrying his cousin, and he couldn't leave an unprotected wean behind.

"Patrick," he said softly, watching the boys advance. "Get tae the hoose! Get yer Ma!"

"We're playing," Patrick replied. "I dinnae want tae go the noo!"

"Dae it, Patrick! Get!"

"Naw!" Patrick yelled back, his little chin trembling. "Why urye making me go in?"

"Please, Patrick! Get in! The noo!"

"I don't want tae play any mere!" the four-year-

158

old spat. "I'm telling Ma you're being right mean tae me!"

"Go tell her! Get out of here, ya wee scunner! Now!"

With that, Patrick ran toward the house, wailing.

The three older boys stopped about a metre from Callum.

"You a hard man, then?" one of them asked.

Callum recognized the school uniforms they wore — he had played football against their school. Callum had started off in his uniform, but had taken off his jacket and tie to play with his cousin.

"He asked a question!" another asked, leaning in close to Callum. He could smell tobacco on his foul breath. He looked closer at Callum. "I know you, don't I? You're the wee bastart that fouled me a month ago."

"You fouled me," said Callum defiantly. "I was just showing you how it felt."

"You're the one who thnks he's a real hot-shot, aren't ye. Showing your fancy tricks afore the game." The boy grinned at him. "I think I have to show you a few tricks of my own.

"Just get on with it," Callum said. He was fast, he knew it. The fastest on his team. He still had a chance to get away. But out of the corner of his eye he saw that his cousin hadn't gone inside. Patrick was on the stairs, peering through the railings.

"You taking the piss?" the first thug asked. He held a large, empty Irn Bru bottle in his hand, smacking it against the open palm of his other hand.

Callum swore and pushed past them, hoping that he could break free, hoping that Patrick would run upstairs. He slipped the football onto his foot and, with a quick true movement, knocked it to knee height before kicking it hard with the side of his foot. The ball hit the first boy square in the face, and blood pooled immediately from his broken nose.

Callum saw this as he felt his feet slip out from under him on the wet grass — he was wearing his leather school shoes, not his cleats. As he fell, quickly rolling onto his back, ready to kick, to bite, to do whatever he could to fight them off, he saw the clear glass of the pop bottle glint in the dull Glasgow sun an instant before it came down on the side of his head.

***

The wean was greeting.

Callum could barely hear him at first, but the crying got louder. He tried to remember what had happened, where he was. The wean was shaking him awake, calling his name. He lifted his head and slowly opened his eyes. They were sticky and it hurt to open them. The sunlight streaming through trees burned his eyes through the closed lids. He tried to lift his hand to shade his eyes and a sudden stab of intense pain made him scream out loud.

Patrick screamed too, tears streaking his dusty cheeks.

"Callum!" his cousin screamed. "Get up! Get up, afore they come back!"

Callum had laid his arm down again, afraid that moving would bring back the intense pain. He looked past his cousin, trying to see where he was. He began to recognize familiar objects, the trees and bushes hanging over him, rustling in the gentle breeze. He heard the sound of a neighbour's greyhound barking. He slowly and carefully looked to his right. He saw the rust-coloured bricks of his own house, saw the back court only a few feet or so away.

"Patrick," Callum said softly, hardly more than a whisper. "Get my Ma."

"Ah cannie, Callum. I won't go. Ah'm too feart!"

"You have tae."

"Ah won't leave you!"

Callum realized he was lying on the wet grass. He looked down and saw that his red shirt was soaked, clinging to his thin body. He saw it was pulled out of the grey flannel pants of his school uniform.

Why did I wear a red shirt to school? he wondered.

Another wave of pain washed over him and he

turned to his little cousin, ready to tell him again to find help. As he sat up slightly, using his elbows as leverage, it felt as though the air was sucked from his lungs. He couldn't breathe. He reached out to his terrified cousin who shrank back from the touch of his red hand.

Callum lay back down, gasping for breath. It felt as though a tonne weight was pressing on his chest. He felt the earth beneath him slowly warm as something wet drained into it. There was a sharp pain in his right leg. He looked down, chest heaving, each breath coming at a terrible cost.

His leg was lying across a small dip in the field. As his eyes focused he saw that it was lying at a weird angle, that his grey flannel pants were ripped, and that something white and meaty protruded through the cloth. He moved his knee slightly. The pain made him scream until the blackness swallowed him again.

**

"Son? Can you hear me?"

Callum opened his eyes to see a red-haired woman in a dark uniform lean over him.

"What?" he said. There was no pain, but he felt disoriented, floating. There was a strange ringing in his ears.

He looked around, saw his mother and aunt kneeling beside him, tears flowing. He saw his little cousin Patrick in his mother's arms, crying

162

nearly hysterically. Callum tried to lift his arm, to comfort his little cousin, but the pain rushed in again and he realized he could still hardly breathe.

It was insane — he lay there under an open sky, smelling the grass and the coming rain, and he couldn't breathe.

"Lie back," the red-haired woman said. He lay back.

"Try to keep still the noo," she said to him. He lay still, even though it felt as though the lead weight was still pressing down on his lungs. The red-haired woman pulled a huge syringe from a bag and ripped open his wet, red shirt. He almost laughed — the syringe was just a plastic tube with no needle attached. *How is she going to give me my medicine*, he wondered.

"This is going to sting, but you'll be able to breathe again," she said.

She placed the needle over the seeping gash over his ribs and pushed.

Callum screamed as the syringe plunged into his chest. But as the woman pushed the plunger, he felt his lung suddenly expand, and he could breathe once more.

The red-haired woman touched his cheek and leaned close to him.

"You're okay, son," said. "A wee bit more to go and we'll have you on your way. Are you ready?"

Callum nodded, thinking the red-haired woman was kind of pretty. A man wearing the same uniform appeared behind the red-haired woman. Callum caught a glimpse of a strange, narrow bed on wheels before the man and the red-haired woman kneeled on either side of him. They nodded at each other as they slipped their hands under Callum's ribs, touching his wet, red shirt, his shirt that should have been white.

They lifted him up, and he had a chance to glance at the pretty woman and the slate-grey Glasgow sky before the pain shot through every nerve, every cell of his body. He screamed and screamed until the darkness took him yet again.

Chapter 16

The small rented moving van waited at the curb, its engine running, as Callum and his parents walked down the small path from his brother's house.

Ewan and Vickie followed close behind, arms wrapped around each other.

Ewan and his father climbed into the cab of the truck. Vickie's small sedan was running on the street behind it, warming up after an October Winnipeg cold snap had left knee-deep snow.

Callum and his parents found a house on the other side of town, a home of their own at last. Callum was glad to be moving away from this street, away from the misery of the last few weeks.

"Looks like you finally got that growth spurt," Vickie said, grinning up at him. He was finally taller than she was. "I'm glad you talked them out of leaving," she said. He nodded and smiled, then hugged her.

Callum saw Aidan waiting for him, leaning against a tree. He was wearing a thick coat and a weird-looking knit cap with long drawstrings.

"Hey," Callum said, waving slightly and approaching his friend.

Aidan stood up straight.

"Hey," Aidan shoved his hands in the pockets of his coat and looked nervous. "So, you're off, huh?"

"Looks like it," Callum said.

"Too bad you couldn't get a place closer to here."

Callum shrugged again. "Too many bad memories. At least it's not Glasgow."

His mother had wanted to go back to Scotland, to a remote village, anywhere to keep her son safe.

"I don't want to run away," Callum had finally told her. "I'm tired of running, tired of being afraid."

And when he had seen his father nod, he knew he felt the same way. So, they compromised. A fresh start in their new country.

As Callum turned to go, Aidan stopped him with, "Hey. You miss her?"

Callum turned to face him. "Every day."

Aidan nodded. "Me, too."

"How's Tyler doing?"

"Okay. He's still grounded. He's real sorry about how he acted."

Callum nodded and turned away with a final wave.

As he sat in the front seat of Vickie's car, he heard his mother humming softly to herself in the back. He looked out the window at the bare trees, the slate-grey skies that looked to snow again at any minute. He closed his eyes as they passed Cindy's house. He didn't want to see it closed tight, the tilted realtors sign, the sign above it announcing *"NEW LOWER PRICE! "*

The cab turned right onto Osborne. Callum pulled his hood over his eyes and sank into the seat, hoping for some rest.

Marquis Book Printing Inc.

Québec, Canada
2007